D0047549

Journal
OF THE
Gun Years

Being CHOICE selections
from the *Authentic*,
never-before-printed
DIARY of the famous
gunfighter-lawman
CLAY HALSER!
whose deeds of *daring*
made his name a by-word
of TERROR in the Southwest
between the YEARS OF
1866 and 1876!

Richard Matheson

FORGE®

A TOM DOHERTY ASSOCIATES BOOK
NEW YORK

JOURNAL OF THE GUN YEARS

Copyright © 1991 by RXR, Inc.

Originally published in 1991 by M. Evans and Company.

A Forge Book
Published by Tom Doherty Associates, LLC
175 Fifth Avenue
New York, NY 10010

www.tor-forge.com

Forge® is a registered trademark of Tom Doherty Associates, LLC.

ISBN-13: 978-0-7653-6226-1
ISBN-10: 0-7653-6226-0

First Forge Edition: May 2009

Printed in the United States of America

0 9 8 7 6 5 4 3 2 1

For:

William Campbell Gault, William R. Cox, Henry Kuttner, Les Savage, Jr., Joe Brennan, Hal Braham, Malden Grange Bishop, Chick Coombs, Dean Owens, Bill Fay, Willard Temple, Frank Bonham, Todhunter Ballard, Wilbur S. Peacock, and all my other friends in the Fictioneers.

Happy memories.

BOOK ONE

(1864-1867)

It is my unhappy lot to write the closing entry in this journal.

Clay Halser is dead, killed this morning in my presence.

I have known him since we met during the latter days of The War Between The States. I have run across him, on occasion, through ensuing years and am, in fact, partially responsible (albeit involuntarily) for a portion of the legend which has magnified around him.

It is for these reasons (and another more important) that I make this final entry.

I am in Silver Gulch acquiring research matter toward the preparation of a volume on the history of this territory (Colorado), which has recently become the thirty-eighth state of our Union.

I was having breakfast in the dining room of the *Silver Lode Hotel* when a man entered and sat down at a table across the room, his back to the wall. Initially, I failed to recognize him though there was, in his comportment, something familiar.

Several minutes later (to my startlement), I realized that it was none other than Clay Halser. True, I had not laid eyes on him for many years. Nonetheless, I was completely taken aback by the change in his appearance.

I was not, at that point, aware of his age, but took it to be somewhere in the middle thirties. Contrary to this, he presented the aspect of a man at least a decade older.

His face was haggard, his complexion (in my memory, quite ruddy) pale to the point of being ashen. His eyes, formerly suffused with animation, now looked burned out, dead. What many horrific sights those eyes had beheld I could not—and cannot—begin to estimate. Whatever those sights, however, no evidence of them had been reflected in his eyes before; it was as though he'd been emotionally immune.

He was no longer so. Rather, one could easily imagine that his eyes were gazing, in that very moment, at those bloody sights, dredging from the depths within his mind to which he'd relegated them, all their awful measure.

From the standpoint of physique, his deterioration was equally marked. I had always known him as a man of vigorous health, a condition necessary to sustain him in the execution of his harrowing duties. He was not a tall man; I would gauge his height at five feet ten inches maximum, perhaps an inch or so less, since his upright carriage and customary dress of black suit, hat, and boots might have afforded him the look of standing taller than he did. He had always been extremely well-presented though, with a broad chest, narrow waist, and pantherlike grace of movement; all in all, a picture of vitality.

Now, as he ate his meal across from me, I felt as though, by some bizarre transfigurement, I was gazing at an old man.

He had lost considerable weight and his dark suit (it, too, seemed worn and past its time) hung loosely on his frame. To my further disquiet, I noted a threading of gray through his dark blond hair and saw a tremor in his hands completely foreign to the young man I had known.

I came close to summary departure. To my shame, I nearly chose to leave rather than accost him. Despite the congenial relationship I had enjoyed with him throughout the past decade, I found myself so totally dismayed by the alteration in his looks that I lacked the will to rise and cross the room to him, preferring to consider a hasty exit. (I discovered, later, that the reason he had failed to notice me was that his vision, always so acute before, was now inordinately weak.)

At last, however, girding up my will, I stood and moved across the dining room, attempting to fix a smile of pleased surprise on my lips and hoping he would not be too aware of my distress.

"Well, good morning, Clay," I said, as evenly as possible.

I came close to baring my deception at the outset for, as he looked up sharply at me, his expression one of taut alarm, a perceptible "tic" under his right eye, I was hard put not to draw back apprehensively.

Abruptly, then, he smiled (though it was more a ghost of the smile I remembered). "*Frank*," he said and jumped to his feet. No, that is not an accurate description of his movement. It may well have been his intent to jump up and welcome me with an avid handshake. As it happened, his stand was labored, his hand grip lacking in strength. "How *are* you?" he inquired. "It is good to see you."

"I'm fine," I answered.

"Good." He nodded, gesturing toward the table. "Join me."

I hope my momentary hesitation passed his notice. "I'd be happy to," I told him.

"Good," he said again.

We each sat down, he with his back toward the wall again. As we did, I noted how his gaunt frame slumped into the chair, so different from the movement of his earlier days.

He asked me if I'd eaten breakfast.

"Yes." I pointed across the room. "I was finishing when you entered."

"I am glad you came over," he said.

There was a momentary silence. Uncomfortable, I tried to think of something to say.

He helped me out. (I wonder, now, if it was deliberate; if he had, already, taken note of my discomfort.) "Well, old fellow," he asked, "what brings you to this neck of the woods?"

I explained my presence in Silver Gulch and, as I did, being now so close to him, was able to distinguish, in detail, the astounding metamorphosis which time (and experience) had effected.

There seemed to be, indelibly impressed on his still handsome face, a look of unutterable sorrow. His former blitheness had completely vanished and it was oppressive to behold what had occurred to his expression, to see the palsied gestures of his hands as he spoke, perceive the constant shifting of his eyes as though he was anticipating that, at any second, some impending danger might be thrust upon him.

I tried to coerce myself not to observe these things, concentrating on the task of bringing him "up to date" on my activities since last we'd met; no match for his activities, God knows.

"What about you?" I finally asked; I had no more to say about myself. "What are you doing these days?"

"Oh, gambling," he said, his listless tone indicative of his regard for that pursuit.

"No marshaling anymore?" I asked.

He shook his head. "Strictly the circuit," he answered.

"Circuit?" I wasn't really curious but feared the onset of silence and spoke the first word that occurred to me.

"A league of boomtown havens for faro players," he replied. "South Texas up to South Dakota—Idaho to Arizona. There is money to be gotten everywhere. Not that I am good enough to make a raise. And not that it's important if I do, at any rate. I only gamble for something to do."

All the time he spoke, his eyes kept shifting, searching; was it *waiting*?

As silence threatened once again, I quickly spoke. "Well, you have traveled quite a long road since the War," I said. "A long, exciting road." I forced a smile. "*Adventurous*," I added.

His answering smile was as sadly bitter and exhausted as any I have ever witnessed. "Yes, the writers of the stories have made it all sound very colorful," he said. He leaned back with a heavy sigh, regarding me. "I even thought it so myself at one time. Now I recognize it all for what it was." There was a tightening around his eyes. "Frank, it was drab, and dirty, and there was a lot of blood."

I had no idea how to respond to that and, in spite of my resolve, let silence fall between us once more.

Silence broke in a way that made my flesh go cold. A young man's voice behind me, from some distance in the room. "So that is him," the voice said loudly. "Well, he does not look like much to me."

I'd begun to turn when Clay reached out and gripped my arm. "Don't bother looking," he instructed me. "It's best to ignore them. I have found the more attention paid, the more difficult they are to shake in the long run."

He smiled but there was little humor in it. "Don't be concerned," he said. "It happens all the time. They spout a while, then go away, and brag that Halser took their guff and never did a thing. It makes them feel important. I don't mind. I've grown accustomed to it."

At which point, the boy—I could now tell, from the timbre of his voice, that he had not attained his majority—spoke again.

"He looks like nothing at all to me to be so all-fired famous a fighter with his guns," he said.

I confess the hostile quaver of his voice unsettled me. Seeing my reaction, Clay smiled and was about to speak when the boy—perhaps seeing the smile and angered by it—added, in a tone resounding enough to be heard in the lobby, "In fact, I believe he looks like a woman-hearted coward, that is what he looks like to me!"

"Don't worry now," Clay reassured me. "He'll blow himself out of steam presently and crawl away." I felt some sense of relief to see a glimmer of the old sauce in his eyes. "Probably to visit, with uncommon haste, the nearest outhouse."

Still, the boy kept on with stubborn malice. "My name is Billy Howard," he announced. "And I am going to make . . ."

He went abruptly mute as Clay unbuttoned his dark frock coat to reveal a butt-reversed Colt at his left side. It was little wonder. Even I, a friend of Clay's, felt a chill of premonition at the movement. What spasm of dread it must have caused in the boy's heart, I can scarcely imagine.

"Sometimes I have to go this far," Clay told me. "Usually I wait longer but, since you are with me . . ." He let the sentence go unfinished and lifted his cup again.

I wanted to believe the incident was closed but, as we spoke—me asking questions to distract my mind from its foreboding state—I seemed to feel the presence of the boy behind me like some constant wraith.

"How are all your friends?" I asked.

"Dead," Clay answered.

"*All* of them?"

He nodded. "Yes. Jim Clements. Ben Pickett. John Harris." I saw a movement in his throat. "Henry Blackstone. All of them."

I had some difficulty breathing. I kept expecting to hear the boy's voice again. "What about your wife?" I asked.

"I have not heard from her in some time," he replied. "We are estranged."

"How old is your daughter now?"

"Three in January," he answered, his look of sadness deepening. I regretted having asked and quickly said, "What about your family in Indiana?"

"I went back to visit them last year," he said. "It was a waste."

I did not want to know, but heard myself inquiring nonetheless, "Why?"

"Oh . . . what I have become," he said. "What journalists have made me. Not you," he amended, believing, I suppose, that he'd insulted me. "My reputation, I mean. It stood like a wall between my family and me. I don't think they saw me. Not *me*. They saw what they believed I am."

The voice of Billy Howard made me start. "Well, why does he just *sit* there?" he said.

Clay ignored him. Or, perhaps, he did not even hear, so deep was he immersed in black thoughts.

"Hickok was right," he said, "I am not a man anymore. I'm a figment of imagination. Do you know, I looked at my reflection in the mirror this morning and did not even know who I was looking at? Who is that staring at me? I wondered. Clay Halser of Pine Grove? Or the *Hero of The Plains*?" he finished with contempt.

"*Well?*" demanded Billy Howard. "Why *does* he?"

Clay was silent for a passage of seconds and I felt my muscles drawing in, anticipating God knew what.

"I had no answer for my mirror," he went on then. "I have no answers left for anyone. All I know is that I am tired. They have offered me the job of City Marshal here and, although I could use the money, I cannot find it in myself to accept."

Clay Halser stared into my eyes and told me quietly, "To answer your long-time question: yes, Frank, I have learned what fear is. Though not fear of . . ."

He broke off as the boy spoke again, his tone now venomous. "I think he is afraid of me," said Billy Howard.

Clay drew in a long, deep breath, then slowly shifted his gaze to look across my shoulder. I sat immobile, conscious of an air of tension in the entire room now, everyone waiting with held breath.

"That is what I think," the boy's voice said. "I think Almighty God Halser is afraid of me."

Clay said nothing, looking past me at the boy. I did not dare to turn. I sat there, petrified.

"I think the Almighty God Halser is a yellow skunk!" cried Billy Howard. "I think he is a murderer who shoots men in the back and will not . . . !"

The boy's voice stopped again as Clay stood so abruptly that I felt a painful jolting in my heart. "I'll be right back," he said.

He walked past me and, shuddering, I turned to watch. It had grown so deathly still in the room that, as I did, the legs of my chair squeaked and caused some nearby diners to start.

I saw, now, for the first time, Clay Halser's challenger and was aghast at the callow look of him. He could not have been more than sixteen years of age and might well have been younger, his face speckled with skin blemishes, his dark hair long and shaggy. He was poorly dressed and had an old six-shooter pushed beneath the waistband of his faded trousers.

I wondered vaguely whether I should move, for I was sitting in whatever line of fire the boy might direct. I wondered vaguely if the other diners were wondering the same thing. If they were, their limbs were as frozen as mine.

I heard every word exchanged by the two.

"Now don't you think that we have had enough of this?" Clay said to the boy. "These folks are having their breakfast and I think that we should let them eat their meal in peace."

"Step out into the street then," said the boy.

"Now why should I step out into the street?" Clay asked. I knew it was no question. He was doing what he could to calm the agitated boy—that agitation obvious as the boy replied, "To fight me with your gun."

"You don't want to fight me," Clay informed him. "You would just be killed and no one would be better for it."

"You mean *you* don't want to fight *me*," the youth retorted. Even from where I sat, I could see that his face was almost white; it was clear that he was terror-stricken.

Still, he would not allow himself to back off, though Clay was giving him full opportunity. "*You* don't want to fight *me*," he repeated.

"That is not the case at all," Clay replied. "It is just that I am tired of fighting."

"I *thought* so!" cried the boy with malignant glee.

"Look," Clay told him quietly, "if it will make you feel good, you are free to tell your friends, or anyone you choose, that I backed down from you. You have my permission to do that."

"I don't need your d——d permission," snarled the boy. With a sudden move, he scraped his chair back, rising to his feet. Unnervingly, he seemed to be gaining resolution rather than losing it—as though, in some way, he sensed the weakness in Clay, despite the fact that Clay was famous for his prowess with the handgun. "I am sick of listening to you," he declared. "Are you going to step outside with me and pull your gun like a man, or do I shoot you down like a dog?"

"Go *home*, boy," Clay responded—and I felt an icy grip of premonition strike me full force as his voice broke in the middle of a word.

"Pull, you yellow b——d," Billy Howard ordered him.

Several diners close to them lunged up from their tables, scattering for the lobby. Clay stood motionless.

"I said *pull*, you God d——d son of a b——h!" Billy Howard shouted.

"No," was all Clay Halser answered.

"Then *I* will!" cried the boy.

Before his gun was halfway from the waistband of his trousers, Clay's had cleared its holster. Then—with what capricious twist of fate!—his shot misfired and, before he could squeeze off another, the boy's gun had discharged and a bullet struck Clay full in the chest, sending him reeling back to hit a table, then sprawl sideways to the floor.

Through the pall of dark smoke, Billy Howard gaped down at his victim. "I did it," he muttered. "I *did* it." Though chance alone had done it.

Suddenly, his pistol clattered to the floor as his fingers lost their holding power and, with a cry of what he likely thought was victory, he bolted from the room. (Later, I heard, he was killed in a knife fight over a poker game somewhere near Bijou Basin.)

By then, I'd reached Clay, who had rolled onto his back, a dazed expression on his face, his right hand pressed against the blood-pumping wound in the center of his chest. I shouted for someone to get a doctor, and saw some man go dashing toward the lobby. Clay attempted to sit up, but did not have the strength, and slumped back.

Hastily, I knelt beside him and removed my coat to form a pillow underneath his head, then wedged my handkerchief between his fingers and the wound. As I did, he looked at me as though I were a stranger. Finally, he blinked and, to my startlement, began to chuckle. "The one time I di . . ." I could not make out the rest. "What, Clay?" I asked distractedly, wondering if I should try to stop the bleeding in some other way.

He chuckled again. "The one day I did not reload," he repeated with effort. "Ben would laugh at that."

He swallowed, then began to make a choking noise, a trickle of blood issuing from the left-hand corner of his mouth. "Hang on," I said, pressing my hand to his shoulder. "The doctor will be here directly."

He shook his head with several hitching movements. "No sawbones can remove me from *this* tight," he said.

He stared up at the ceiling now, his breath a liquid sound

that made me shiver. I did not know what to say, but could only keep directing worried (and increasingly angry) glances toward the lobby. "Where *is* he?" I muttered.

Clay made a ghastly, wheezing noise, then said, "My God." His fingers closed in, clutching at the already blood-soaked handkerchief. "I am going to die." Another strangling breath. "And I am only thirty-one years old."

Instant tears distorted my vision. *Thirty-one?*

Clay murmured something I could not hear. Automatically, I bent over and he repeated, in a labored whisper, "She was such a pretty girl."

"Who?" I asked; could not help but ask.

"Mary Jane," he answered. He could barely speak by then. Straightening up, I saw the grayness of death seeping into his face and knew that there were only moments left to him.

He made a sound which might have been a chuckle had it not emerged in such a hideously bubbling manner. His eyes seemed lit now with some kind of strange amusement. "I could have married her," he managed to say. "I could still be there." He stared into his fading thoughts. "Then I would never have . . ."

At which his stare went lifeless and he expired.

I gazed at him until the doctor came. Then the two of us lifted his body—how *frail* it was—and placed it on a nearby table. The doctor closed Clay's eyes and I crossed Clay's arms on his chest after buttoning his coat across the ugly wound. Now he looked almost at peace, his expression that of a sleeping boy.

Soon people began to enter the dining room. In a short while, everyone in Silver Gulch, it seemed, had heard about Clay's death and come running to view the remains. They shuffled past his impromptu bier in a double line, gazed at him and, ofttimes, murmured some remark about his life and death.

As I stood beside the table, looking at the gray, still features, I wondered what Clay had been about to say before the rancorous voice of Billy Howard had interrupted. He'd said that he had learned what fear is, "though not fear of . . ."

What words had he been about to say? Though not fear of
other men? Of danger? Of death?

Later on, the undertaker came and took Clay's body after I
had guaranteed his payment. That done, I was requested, by
the manager of the hotel, to examine Clay's room and see
to the disposal of his meager goods. This I did and will return
his possessions to his family in Indiana.

With one exception.

In a lower bureau drawer, I found a stack of Record Books
bound together with heavy twine. They turned out to be a
journal which Clay Halser kept from the latter part of the
War to this very morning.

It is my conviction that these books deserve to be published. Not in their entirety, of course; if that were done, I estimate the book would run in excess of a thousand pages.
Moreover, there are many entries which, while perhaps of interest to immediate family (who will, of course, receive the
Record Books when I have finished partially transcribing
them), contribute nothing to the main thrust of his account,
which is the unfoldment of his life as a nationally recognized
lawman and gunfighter.

Accordingly, I plan to eliminate those sections of the journal which chronicle that variety of events which any man
might experience during twelve years' time. After all, as hair-
raising as Clay's life was, he could not possibly exist on the
razor edge of peril every day of his life. As proof of this, I will
incorporate a random sampling of those entries which may be
considered, from a "thrilling" standpoint, more mundane.

In this way—concentrating on the sequences of "action"—
it is hoped that the general reader, who might otherwise ignore the narrative because of its unwieldy length, will more
willingly expose his interest to the life of one whom another
journalist has referred to as "The Prince of Pistoleers."

Toward this end, I will, additionally, attempt to make cor-
rections in the spelling, grammar and, especially, punctuation
of the journal, leaving, as an indication of this necessity, the
opening entry. It goes without saying that subsequent entries
need less attention to this aspect since Clay Halser learned,

by various means, to read and write with more skill in his later years.

I hope the reader will concur that, while there might well be a certain charm in viewing the entries precisely as Clay Halser wrote them, the difficulty in following his style through virtually an entire book would make the reading far too difficult. It is for this reason that I have tried to simplify his phraseology without—I trust—sacrificing the basic flavor of his language.

Keep in mind, then, that if the chronology of this account is, now and then, sporadic (with occasional truncated entries), it is because I have used, as its main basis, Clay Halser's life as a man of violence. I hope, by doing this, that I will not unbalance the impression of his personality. While trying not to intrude unduly on the texture of the journal, I may occasionally break into it if I believe my observations may enable the reader to better understand the protagonist of what is probably the bloodiest sequence of events to ever take place on the American frontier.

I plan to do all this, not for personal encomiums, but because I hope that I may be the agency by which the public-at-large may come to know Clay Halser's singular story, perhaps to thrill at his exploits, perhaps to moralize but, hopefully, to profit by the reading for, through the page-by-page transition of this man from high-hearted exuberance to hopeless resignation, we may, perhaps, achieve some insight into a sad, albeit fascinating and exciting, phenomenon of our times.

Frank Leslie
April 19, 1876

September 12, 1864

We are still here in this Valley, I think we will be here For
Ever with those Secesh Boys keep us boteled up, the Sholder
Strapps say we are at a Place called Al Mans Swich wer ever
that is, I do not no, all I *Do* no is the Army of the Patomic is
siting here, siting here and those Secesh Boys piking us of
like Pigins on a log, I hate siting, siting, I feel tyd down like a
prisner and I wish we just *Go*!! I hate to feel tyd down, by
G————. I hate it! I think if we woud Go and Go Hard we
woud thro those Jony Rebs back to Jef Davis Back Porch, that
woud be the *End* of it, I rely feel that, *Do* it, *Do* it, dont just
Sit Here like lumps, we her to suport the Artilery but all we
are suporting our own rer ends while we *Sit* here!! Why think
it all out, just GO!!!

My frend from New Jersy Albirt Jonson (I think that is a
rong speling his Last Name) he took a Minie Ball in the rigt
side this afternoon, it put him in grate pain, was holering and
crying Some Thing awfil that I did feel sorry for him he was
feeling so bad, it must have hurt like H————, poor Albirt.
So a few of us Boys caried him Behind The Lines, we finily
fond a waggin going North and placed him on it, caried him
away poor fello, he was bleding Some Thing ferce, I hope he
makes it—And as if that was not enogh the salt beef and
patatos gave us last nigt made a bunch siker than Dogs, how
we did "cast up acounts" over the Hill Side and down the
Creek was Some Thing awfil! How Ever at the start I did not
feel sik but as more and more my comrads got sik after a time
I did to and went the same road.

It did not make me feel beter to get a note from Mother, you
woud think I took a trip for pursonel plesur here in Vergina

insted of figting a D———War! Why doesnt She leave me be
not alway Scolding me as poring linamint into a sore with
Ever Lasting Heranging, why did I leve the Farm when there
is so much Work to do there, why did I enlist in the Army of
the Patomic when there are lots of soldirs who can figt the
War but No, no, no "Not enogh Good Men At Home" to help
take care of ther Familes, My Lord She goes on and on and
on, no wonder He went off to California (My Father) I think
the Army of The Secesh less to face than *Her*, I mean I Rispect
her and all but why does She never stop Heranging me, I am
in a D———War for G———'s sake, not for pursonel
plesure!! Well that is that and we had beter move soon or I
take my Rifel and go at those Rebs all my self and mean so in
Ernest!!

September 14, 1864

Yesterday, this time, I thought we would be here forever. The
problem this way: the Secesh Army planted solid on the
Heights and regardless how our batteries fired at them—our
cannons burning hot!—were so much dug in it did no good at
all. This is a "key spot" Lieutenant Hale said; the Rebels need
to hold it At Any Cost and no matter what we did, they held.

We started rushing them, charging the heights, bayonets in
fix position, but a volley of fire burned at us and we were
forced back in defeat, half dead and wounded on the field.
Only our artillery at them saved any at all though it did hit
some of our boys too. It was a bloody attack that was no use.
I had 60 rounds of lead pills which, when it was over, I was
down to 17 and I do not know if I had hit a soul, the smoke
so heavy you could not see through it the boys in Grey were
hid so.

At three o'clock this afternoon Lieutenant Hale collected a
group—eight in all—and led us up the far slope of the Valley
to "harass" the enemy. He said, "Come on, boys! Today we
have a chance to fight our way to Glory!"

He was right, we *did*! It was a battle out of H————but I came out without a scratch. I think my life is charmed because, when we charged up that slope, though it was far to one side, shot and shell ploughed up the ground in all directions; it was flying hot and heavy. Minnie Balls were buzzing all around us like swarms of angry bees! I felt the *wind* of them and some went by my ears so close they made me jump but not a one could touch me!

By when we reached the top, there was only three remaining, George Havers, me and some fat man from New York State that I had not met. (How he climbed that slope not being blown to his Maker I will never know!) We got behind a fallen tree and, from that point, through clouds of smoke, could see the Grey lines clear as day. I said to Havers and the fat man we must fire at the Secesh batteries, but they were none too keen to lift their heads as bombarding shot was fierce and Southern Sharp Shooters doing their best to kill us!

So I had to do it my self though Havers, to admit the truth, did fire a shot or two. Mostly, it was me how ever and the first time I got value from the Sharps I picked up last month from the body of a killed Confederate. Lord All Mighty, how that piece can do! I aimed first for the Sharp Shooters, those I could see, and it was like I could not miss. I had 30 lead pills in my sack and there were not too many wasted! I shot at Battery Crews I saw and they fell also; Rebs were going down like sitting birds! I lost count at twelve what with smoke and noise and being worked up, I fell in what you might say was half sleep. I kept firing and firing and Havers screamed, "God, boy, you hit *another*! God, boy, you hit *another*!"

When the firing at our lines grew thin, our boys came charging up and took the Heights and it was all because of me that we could whip them! Now they are on the run and I am happy as a clam at high water! I can say it if I want, no one will read this.

That is for now. I am glad I took this Record Book from a dead Rebel officer last week. I believe I will keep writing in it regular because . . .

Jim Brockmuller told me some boys have come across a Moonshine Still the Greys were running so there is going to be a lot of Liquid Joy tonight!

September 16, 1864

Early morning—the boys are sleeping off the battle for the Moonshine Whiskey Heights. I believe our officers were wise to let us drink after what we went through yesterday; anyway more fellows came to drink than expected—good news does travel fast!—and no one got enough to hear the owl hoot. It made our bellies warm though and our heads some light.

I can not sleep for thinking of the man I met last night. His name is Frank Leslie, a Reporter for *The New York Ledger*. He had heard about my part in the battle and came to ask questions to write about it in his News paper. I can not get over it. A story in a News paper read by thousands. About *me*. The folks in Pine Grove will be some surprised to read it, I imagine. Specially Mother: may be she will sing a warmer song now. And Mary Jane. It thrills me to think about her reading what I did. I would not show her this Record Book (or show it to any one) but if a News paper man wants to write about me I can not stop him. So long as I do not have to see or talk to all those people who read it; I want to be *Private* Halser all the way. But I do not object to a story in a News paper.

After he had introduced him self to me, Mr. Leslie said that several of the boys had "witnessed my heroic action" (as he put it) specially Private George Havers, Mill Town, Pennsylvania; that was nice of George, I thanked him later.

"He tells me that you turned the tide of battle almost single-handedly." Those were his words. It happened that I shot down nineteen Rebels, killing eleven including two officers, "throwing such confusion and dismay into the Southern ranks that they began to waver," as Mr. Leslie stated it. (I wrote down that hill of words soon after, so not to forget them.)

"Tell me, Private Halser," Mr. Leslie said. "What were you feeling during that engagement?"

"I was not feeling any thing," I answered. "I had little time for feeling."

"You felt no fear?" he asked me with surprise.

"No, sir," I told him. I explained that I do not know what that particular "emotion" feels like; he was even more surprised to hear that. May be I am odd, I fail to know. I was not even able to "build up" what I did. I suppose that was a dumb thing but I did not want to lie to him; not for a News paper. I had to tell him, in all truth, that I have had a lot of targets more hard to hit in my life. I agree they were not shooting back (which counts for *something*) but they were a H———— of a lot smaller and moving faster.

"To what do you refer?" he asked. Lord, to talk so savory!

I told him when I was a boy in Pine Grove (that made him smile because I believe he thinks I look like a boy now, though nineteen) I had to supply my family with meat, my father being dead. (I did not reveal the truth about Father as I do not believe Mother would be pleased to see it printed in a News paper.) Any way, with five brothers and one sister plus Mother that was some degree of meat to provide. So I had to learn to shoot All Mighty Straight All Mighty Soon or we would starve to death once Father was gone. Specially with the cock-eyed Ballard I had to use; it drifted like a d———— boat!

I told him how I learned to shoot when I was ten. He was right surprised by that. I can still see the expression on his face as he said, *"Ten?"*

"Yes, sir," I answered. "I was small for my age and all the bullies in the country side had them selves a frolic on me. I was black and blue so much some people thought I had a un-known disease."

I went on to tell him that, for Xmas 1855, my Uncle Simon gave me his worn out Maynard for a present and I made use of it first rattle out of the box. I practiced regular and it was some hard doing as well as my chores because I had to keep firing the same lead balls again and again. I did so, how ever, and in not too much time I learned to down a small bird on the wing.

"That was when I gathered all the bullies of the area to watch me shoot," I said to Mr. Leslie. "After that, the black and blue spots started fading."

We talked a while more and, at last, he asked what I planned to do with my self after the war was over. I told him I am not certain save one thing—I will not let my self be tied down but will live a fast, exciting life of some kind, that is for dead sure!

March 9, 1866

Another day gone off where ever days go when they end. It is some hard to recall when life had some excitement. H———, it is some hard to believe it *ever* had excitement. Here I am at home, the farm, the d——— chores—when I do them— Mother at me all the time to do more, do more. I have got to get out of here soon, I *mean* it.

I am sitting by candle light, writing in my Record Book. It started good in the War but is some thing to make a man sleep now. I feel tied down with ropes. I want to get away but Mother tells me (enough times to bury me) there are things I must take care of, I am the man of the house, she needs me, the family needs me, may be if Father had not run off to California—words, words shoveled at me night and day.

I feel my life is wasted. I am stuck here on this d———farm in this d——— community, I agreed to marry Mary Jane come Spring; I do not even know how that took place, I swear I never said the actual words, "Will you marry me?" but, some how, it has happened. I do not know where we would live; Mother no doubt expects on the farm. I would not want that but do not like the thought of trying to work in Pine Grove either. I mean I love Mary Jane and all but feel sick inside to see myself a married man and father growing old in this dead place. What else can I *do* though?

Well this: I am thinking of leaving Pine Grove to go out West. We hear each day, it seems, how much is going on out there. There are new chances and all manner of excitement. I have got to give it serious thought.

March 11, 1866

Just helped Ralph to bed. He is a good lad and I do not think will tell Mother what happened tonight at the *Black Horse Tavern.* It was good luck she was sleeping when we got home or I would be on the taking end of a "word hiding" right now I am certain; not to mention what poor Ralph would have to endure, being younger.

Ralph came to town to fetch me as Mother was angry at my absence all day and knew I was somewhere in Pine Grove drinking and playing cards as I do, so she sent Ralph to bring me back for a "good talking to" as she likes to call it— several hundred times a week.

I was playing Seven Up with several of the boys when Ralph came in. He walked behind my chair and said, "I have been looking for you, Clay."

"Good, you found me," I told him. "Now go home." I had been drinking my fair share of whiskey and, what with losing cards, was feeling not to happy with my lot.

"Mother says she wants you to come home," Ralph said.

"Tell Mother I will come home when I am ready," I responded. "Now get out of here."

The other boys piped in and said the same, for Ralph to clear out, he was ruining the card game.

Ralph is not easy to push, how ever, and kept on ragging me. Mother says the north field needs plowing out for rocks, you promised long ago to do it. Mother says the roof is leaking and one of the windows. Mother says we need meat and on and on.

Finally, he started pulling at my sleeve and riled me proper, so I gave him a shove and he slipped on a wet spot on the floor and landed on his elbow. I guess it hurt something bad for he began to cry even though he is sixteen. At which the boys at the table started jibing him for being a Cry Baby. I told them to "lay off" but they continued doing so.

At this, Ralph got all wrathy—he has the Halser temper like us boys all do—even though he is as skinny as a corn stalk. He jumped up and to the table where he slapped the cards from Bob Fisher's hand, who had been the worst one, pretending to be Ralph and crying like a infant.

This got Bob Fisher good and mad so he got up and, when Ralph had a swing at him that missed, he punched Ralph on the nose and made it bleed.

I could not let that happen to my brother so I dropped my cards and jumped up. Bob turned just in time to get it on the jaw from my fist and go flying back, falling over Ralph.

This made Hannibal Fisher mad to see *his* younger brother hit so he jumped up and hit me on the head. I returned the favor, punching his left eye so he fell across the table we were playing on and knocked the cards and money all to H———.

Every one got wrathy then and I was fighting four of them. Ralph was on my side, I guess, but little help. Every time he tried to give me aid, I got an extra blow or two because he hindered more than helped. I did the best I could, gave my share of hits and bruises, but there were too many what with Ralph no help and soon the two of us flew straight out through the bat wing doors and landed on the street. Ralph had bleeding from his mouth and nose. My head was ringing but I tried to make him stay outside so I could go back in and give a better account of myself, but Ralph insisted he would go along and we would "clean" the place out. I decided it was wiser to forget it, talked him out of it. He is a good lad but a bad joke as a fighter.

It is sad when a tavern dog fight (which I lose) is the best thing I have known in months!

March 14, 1866

I have just come back from Mary Jane's house and feel I have to say I am some low, fiendish being straight from H———!

That poor, sweet Angel of a girl deserves a better fellow than me. I love her dearly and admire her and she is ever kind to me—so why do I feel like a trap is just about to clamp shut on me? What is wrong with me? What is wrong with living here in Pine Grove for that matter? It is . . .

H————and brimstone, I can not even finish that remark! Pine Grove is the dullest, dumbest place on God's Green Earth! I have got to go out West! I need to make my mind up—*do* it! I am not afraid to go, that is not it. It is because I do not want to make Mary Jane unhappy. Not to mention Mother who keeps talking of the wedding all the time now and how Mary Jane and me will share the farm and if I want to I can build a separate house and we will all be together—GOD! The more I think of it, the worse I feel!

Does Mary Jane complain how ever? No, not her. She is so sweet and understanding. She is an *Angel* and I know she had other offers. Why does she want *me*? She is such a fine person yet wants no more than to be Mary Jane Halser, make a happy home for me, bear and raise my children and live her span by my side. What is wrong with that?

I have got to resolve my mind soon. I can not do this to her. Am I the master of my life or not? Do I want a life of excitement or not? *Am I going to go out West or not*?

If only some thing would make up my mind for me.

March 21, 1866

I can not believe it, looking back. It came so sudden and without a hint.

I was in the *Black Horse Tavern* playing Seven Up with several of the boys. Also in the game was Scoby Menlo, son of Truman Menlo, owner of The Pine Grove Mercantile and Shipping. I had not seen much of Scoby since the War but heard he was a hot head and a scoundrel; several of the local girls were got "in trouble" by him and their families paid off by his father.

I soon found out the truth of the report about his temper. I am not the coolest head around but he was worse. I had enjoyed a winning streak and built my pile to more than forty dollars. I was feeling good, thinking Mother would be pleased to see the money; I would claim it was an old loan paid to me or unexpected money from my Army pay.

Menlo was feeling other wise from me. His face got redder as we played. He slammed his cards on the table when he lost, and cursed, and drank his whiskey down like water.

Finally, it came. He glared at me and said, "I think some body at this table cheats at cards."

It did not take a college man to know he meant me since I was the only one who had a winning pile. I tried to ignore it though because I felt so good; I was some whiskey laden as well.

It did not end at that how ever. Shortly later, Menlo spoke again. "No one wins so much at cards unless they cheat," he said.

I could not pretend I did not understand those words and felt a low fire catching in my belly. "If you mean me," I said, "not only are you dead wrong but I want you to apologize for what you said."

He made a snorting noise like that was some joke I had spoken. The fire in my belly rose, I looked him in the eye and told him, "I believe you heard."

He stared at me, his cheeks a little redder now. I noted how his eyes reminded me of Beulah's (our pig) and considered telling him so.

"Yes, I heard," he said.

"Then do what I ask," I said.

"Apologize to you?" he answered with a sneering smile. "A card cheat?"

"You say that one more time," I told him, "and I will wipe the floor with you."

His face looked white now; I recall how fast the color left his cheeks. "Wrong," he said. His voice was shaking. *"I am going to wipe the floor with your blood."*

At that, he unbuttoned the front of his coat so I saw the handle of a six-shooter under his belt. He started reaching for it.

As quick as thought, I knew all talk was ended for there was no point in telling him I was not armed because he meant to kill me where I sat. That so, I leaped up fast and dived across the table at him, grabbing at his right hand and, by fortune, getting it before he could pull the gun free. He fell back on his chair, me on top of him, and we began to wrestle on the floor, he trying hard to get the gun so he might shoot me dead. I said nothing as we struggled for the will to murder was as clear as writing in his eyes.

I do not know how it happened but the gun went off like thunder; still inside his trousers and he screamed in pain. I jerked back and I saw a red stain at his stomach, spreading on his shirt so fast I knew the wound was fatal. Menlo tried to stand but had no strength to do it and he sat down, weak, his right hand over his stomach. He made a sound like he was going to cry. "You b———d," he said. "You killed me."

Moments after, he slumped back on the floor, cold dead.

I stared at him, heart beating so hard it hurt my chest. I had never killed any one face to face and it was terrible to know I had.

No one made a move. I can not guess how long we stood, silent as a cemetery, looking down at Menlo and the puddle of blood around his body.

Then Donald Bell (the bar tender) said some thing about the Constable. At his words, I felt an extra blow of fright inside my heart because I knew Scoby's father having so much power, he would see me hang for sure.

I turned and ran outside to jump on Kit. I rode home in a lather and told Mother what happened. She was no help to me, only saying, "I knew it. I knew it—" following me around the house while I gathered some clothes and my Record Book and flung them in a sack. I told her I had to take Kit but she did not seem to hear my words. She kept saying, "I knew it. I knew it—" like that would help me. I felt sick to hear her so uninterested in what happened and gave up trying to explain.

I did not want to wake my brothers or Nell so kissed their cheeks as they slept and turned away from them. I tried to kiss Mother but she pushed me off, looking angry though tears ran on her cheeks and saying those words again. I came close to tears my self at that. "Well, good bye then!" I shouted. "If that is all I mean to you!"

I wanted to stop at Mary Jane's house to explain what happened but, near Pine Grove, I could see an armed pursuit preparing and was forced to pull the horse around and gallop for the Wabash River.

I have stopped to rest Kit for a while and write this down by moonlight; I will be an easy target if they see me.

God have mercy on me, it is done now. I am off the plank and have to swim alone. I wondered what will happen to me. Will they over take and capture me? Will I hang for Scoby's try.to murder me? Where will I go now?

D———! The answer is so clear, I feel a fool for even wondering.

West!

July 12, 1866

I am in Morgan City, Kansas. I have only the dinero (which means money, I learned) to sleep tonight and buy some food but still feel *good*. This place is Alive! It may be just a dirty trail town but I never saw the like, so Pine Grove seems as far away as Russia!

There is one Main Street. On each side sit saloons, gambling houses, dance halls, cafes, theatres, stables, horse trade corrals, stores, hotels. Not one building looks like it will last a year, all give the feel of being built last week.

And the men and women! Every kind a person could imagine. Cow boys with their Ten Gallon hats, merchants in their white shirts, buffalo hunters in their bloody ones, gamblers in their fancy duds, the street seems never empty of them! Also women like I never saw in Pine Grove. Dance hall girls and actresses and "worse," not many high tones here though you see a few. But I like them all and like this town! It took me long to get here, had to sell my saddle, then sell Kit, work at different jobs but here I am and mean to stay.

I know that I am going to find a life of excitement now!

July 14, 1866

Did not have one shin plaster in my pocket so have taken work in a saloon, *The Red Dog*. I am clean up man and—may be—relief bar tender. It is not what you would call a "fancy" position but beggers can not be choosers—as Mother liked to say—and I am in the begger group all right until I earn some dollars.

The regular bar tender is a tall, thin fellow, Jim Clements by name. He gave me a dollar of his own to find a place to live so I am going to take up in a boarding house run by a Mrs. Kelly, not bad.

I start tonight.

July 16, 1866

I can not believe it! I have seen it happen after only four days here!

I was talking to Jim Clements while behind the bar; just brought out a tray of glasses from washing them. I told him how exciting Morgan City was compared to Pine Grove and he nodded at my words.

"Yes, that is how it is in cow towns," he observed. "All this H——— raising is common because these towns are made so cow boys can blow off steam at the end of cattle drives."

"I never saw so much going on," I said, "not since the War."

And that is G——d's truth! Cow boys crowd the streets by hundreds, some big drive having ended. They fill saloons and gambling houses and what Jim calls "Pleasure Domes"; that is a funny name for crib houses.

"These cow boys have a lot of 'pent up' action in their blood," Jim said. "They want to have them selves a blow out before riding out for more long months of hardship on the plains." He reminds me, by his words, of that reporter in the War, what was his name? I will look it up, hold on.

Frank Leslie.

Any way, we talked on and I told him that I like the West a lot but cow boy life did not appeal to me.

"No, a man has to have a taste for it," Jim admitted.

We went on some more about Morgan City. Since its money comes from "walking beef" as Jim referred to them, and from the men who "walk" them, no one aims to see the town "domesticated" as Jim called it. Even the peace officer is told by Main Street owners not to step on cow boy toes.

His name is Hickok called "Wild Bill." It seems I heard of

him but I am not sure. Jim says he came out from Illinois and was the scout for a General named Custer. Jim says he (Hickok) has built him self a reputation as a man to be accounted for in any "show down." Still he does not make efforts to preserve the peace except for may be outright murder. Which occurs a good bit here, Jim said. "A word and a blow too often turns into a word and a shot—" was how he put it.

And, of all strange things, he said it and—in *seconds*—that very thing took place in front of me!

A big, tall, ugly cow boy started arguing with some man Jim said (later) worked in a livery stable down the street. I could hardly believe what they argued about. Like this—

"And I say cows is stupider—" The cow boy.

"And *I* say *horses*—" The livery stable man.

"Well, what do *you* know?" said the cow boy. "I *live* with the G——— d——— stupid critters and I say horses can read *books* compared to cows!"

"Well, I take *care* of horses night and day and nothing on this whole wide world is dumber than those G——— d——— buzzard heads!" the other man replied.

I thought it all right and funny and was chuckling (so was Jim) when, in a flash, the two men started cursing at each other, then shoving, then the cow boy pulled his gun and shot the livery stable man right in the chest. There was a cloud of dark smoke but I saw the livery man knocked back on the floor. The cow boy fired his gun so close it set the dead man's shirt on fire.

I admit I stood behind the counter like a statue. I know what killing is. I shot those soldiers in the War and, though not intended, had to do with Menlo's death. But that was over *something*; Menlo called me a cheat at cards and made the threat of wiping the floor with my blood. This was over *nothing*, the brains of cows and horses for G———d's sake! Still the livery stable man is no less dead than if there had been reason to it.

Jim has seen this kind of thing before, it was clear: he filled a stein with beer and leaned across the counter to dump it on the dead man's shirt, then did the same again and put the fire out. All the time he did, the ugly cow boy was glaring around like daring any one to say him wrong.

Jim was first to speak. "You better clear out or you'll likely be arrested, charged, and hanged," he said.

The cow boy did not like to hear this; he looked like a red-faced savage, I believe the blood lust had got into him. "Don't tell me to clear out," he said.

"You better pull your freight," Jim told him. His tone was peaceful and did not seem distressed but there was a look in his black eyes that did not mean well for the cow boy, I believed.

The cow boy did not see the look. "I am warning you, you skinny, no account b——d," he said.

"Would you rather I sent for Hickok?" Jim asked.

"Sure, you yellow-livered son of a b——h," the cow boy said. "Get somebody else to help you."

Jim only looked at him. The cow boy had a mean smile; he was full of "forked lightning." "If you had the guts of a pig, you would meet me outside, man to man," he said.

"Is that what you want?" Jim asked.

"Come outside and I will meet you smoking," was the cow boy's answer.

Jim did not reply but reached beneath the counter and picked up a .41 revolver kept in case of someone trying robbery. The cow boy twitched, then stepped back, Jim slipping the gun beneath his waistband and, with no word, heading for the bat wing doors. The cow boy looked some stupid watching; I think he was amazed that Jim accepted him. Then he cursed, and spat, and said "All right!" and swaggered for the doors.

I hurried after them and got a spot outside the door.

It did not last long. Jim and the cow boy stood about nine feet apart on the street off the plank walk, looking at each other. The cow boy said, "You b——d! *Die!*" and grabbed down at his gun. Jim reached for his, the cow boy pulled first but was shaking, I believe. There was a roaring shot from his gun, then another from Jim's and, for moments, I could not see clearly for the cloud of powder smoke. Then I saw the cow boy on his knees, thrown back. He made a sound of pain and fell to his right side, cursing, and dying.

Jim incurred a powder burn across the left sleeve of his shirt. He rubbed it as he walked past me, saying, "Never leave the counter untended." I watched in awe as he returned to his spot and put the .41 away, started pouring whiskey for a customer. He is a chunk of steel and anyone who strikes him will strike fire, that is sure.

I could never be as brave as that.

August 9, 1866

It has been a slow few weeks. I am beginning to think excitement is not ahead of me after all. The job is boring at the *Red Dog*; there is nothing to it which I do not mind but it is dull. If Jim was not there I feel I would move on.

I like him though and believe I can account him as my friend. He does not say much of him self but I have learned he comes from Pennsylvania, fought in the Army of the Potomac, incurred a shrapnel wound at Gettysburg (has a scar on his back, he told me), never married, is a loner.

He is nice to me. I do not know how old he is (thirty-five may be) but he is like a sort of father. He has bought me dinner twice, gives me good advice on how to get by, and there was the day we took that ride together on rented horses I liked a lot.

Still, life in total is dull. I almost feel the way I did in Pine Grove. Morgan City is a wilder place but not that wild; that cow boy thing I saw is all there was. I am twice now to the Golden Temple but did not like the girls each time, they are too rough and out spoken for my taste, also one stole a dollar from me, I am sure. Jim says what can you expect from them?

Now what?

August 11, 1866

Finally some thing different in my life.

Last night was my night off so I went to the Fenway Circus which has stopped in Morgan City. I was much pleased by the chance as I have not done much of pleasure since arrival having to collect hard money after taking part in that game of Black Jack I was lucky to come out of with my teeth.

Any way, I was excited and went running down the street to town edge where the circus was set up. In dashing on the grounds, I bumped into a tall man in a black suit and, as luck would have it, it was no man else but Hickok, a tall fellow with drooping mustache, not bad looking—but what a temper! I thought, first, he was going to shoot me, then kick or hit me but he settled for a "dressing down" my ears have not heard since that Sergeant, training for the War. Hickok has more than guns in his arsenal, he has cuss words in such number and array as few men possess and I believe he used them all on me at once.

I did not like it, made me simmer some but, after all, he is the Marshal and had two guns. I had nothing. If there had been a weapon in my pocket, I might not—H———, what am I saying? I would have "called him out"? Not likely for his pale blue eyes are not too pleasant as they bore at you, so I let him have it out and took it all without a peep. As said, I did not like it, who does to have your skin flayed off by someone's tongue, still what could I do?

When he turned and stormed away from me, I took a breath; which was how I saw a woman nearby, smiling at me. I suppose she saw the whole event. I did not think what to do until she said. "Don't let him bother you. He has a hard job and his nerves are rubbed thin."

At that I smiled back and we introduced our selves. She said her name was Hazel Thatcher, she and her husband are performers with the circus, doing bare back riding. She was fine looking I saw, with a head of red hair very handsome. We had a chat, quite nice, then she held her hand out, said she hoped I would enjoy the show. She seemed to hold my hand a little longer than I would suppose but decided that was imagined.

Enjoy the show I did! Well worth each penny of the dollar and fifty cents though I have little dinero to spare. I confess I spent a good deal of the show looking for the arrival of Hazel Thatcher and, when she arrived, all the time she was performing staring at her in her costume which was less than eyes could believe! She is one grand figure of a woman, that is certain, every curve complete. Her costume, as noted, brief as law will bear and all the men went crazy over her, whistling and stamping; no louder than a certain party in the front row, initials C.H. She is graceful as a bird as well. She and her husband, Carl (mostly her, he seemed less lively), did leaps, and somersaults, and capers on the back of a galloping horse to much thunderlike clapping; my palms were red and stinging after they went off.

Following the performance, I sat a long time in the tent, not wanting to depart, savoring the show like some kind of feast I was digesting. In truth, I hoped (did not admit to my self at first) that Hazel Thatcher would appear so I might tell her I thought she was a fine acrobat and beautiful lady. She never did show up though and, at last, the workers told me to be on my way, they had to "strike" the tent.

I went outside, the grounds were dark and no one anywhere in sight. I strolled across them and, in walking around a wagon, of all things, came upon Hazel Thatcher and her husband. I saw then why his movements were not lively in the show—he was drunk, she leading him, one arm around him; I could smell his breath from feet away.

I felt embarrassed to come on them in that way but Hazel Thatcher seemed pleased to see me, asked right off if I would help her take her husband to their wagon.

I said I would be glad to, grabbed his left arm while she held his right. His legs were made of rubber it appeared and various times he almost fell. He kept muttering, "This is not necessary—" in a kind of dignified voice; but it *was* necessary since he would have toppled if we had not held him up.

"This is very nice of you," Hazel Thatcher told me as we led her husband.

I still was embarrassed. "I am very glad to help," I said.

"This is not necessary," said her husband.

"He has been feeling pain from a broken leg which never healed right," Hazel Thatcher told me. "That is why he drinks a little more than good for him."

I nodded.

"This is not necessary," said her husband as he almost fell again.

It took a while to get him up the steps of their wagon and I wondered how the man was able to perform in such a state until Hazel Thatcher told me he had started drinking heavily after the show was ended and I recalled that I had sat inside the tent long enough for a minister to paint his nose.

At last we got Carl Thatcher on his bunk and he went off to sleep, was snoring in a second. Hazel Thatcher thanked me and I said that I was pleased to be of service, started to back out of the wagon when she asked me to help her light the hanging lantern which I did.

I confess to being raptured by the sight of oil light on her face. Her skin is very white and clear, eyes green as jade with long red hair falling on her shoulders. I have never seen a woman so beautiful in all respects. I stared at her, she smiled and touched my cheek. "You are very handsome," she said.

I had no reply, I felt a stupid boy again. Hazel Thatcher smiled (what teeth!) and asked if I would care to have a cup of coffee with her. Well, to tell the world I would have said "yes" if she asked me if I cared to have a cup of poison with her. "Yes, thank you," I replied.

She told me sit down at the table (very small) and I did while she removed her cloak. She looked around then, I had made a gasping noise because she still had on her costume and the sight of her white shoulders and bosom tops caused me to catch my breath. She smiled at me, leaned over and kissed my cheek (she did!). "You are very sweet and young," she said, those were actual words. I remember shivering though far from cold.

I did not hear her words too well as she prepared the coffee, I was too entranced in looking at her, I mean close up she was so remarkable to look at, she made me feel (the only word that catches it) *hungry*. I did not hear the snoring of her husband which was loud, I was so much fascinated by her looks, the truth is I have never seen the like, not ever.

What did she say? (I said nothing, a staring lump.) I think she said her husband once was a star performer in a Europe circus, drank occasional but not much. His wife was killed in an accident during a performance and he had lost interest in life, began to drink for real because he thought her death his fault. The circus let him go, then another, and he ended up in the United States where he took a job with another circus, his reputation as a bare back rider ahead of his reputation as a drinker, in this country any way.

He kept on drinking and that circus let him go and the next one hiring him was Fenway Circus where he met Hazel Moore (her previous name). They married and, for some while, he seemed better, taught her all the bare back tricks and things looked bright. But he started "hitting at" the whiskey vat again and now is hanging by a thread since he managed to be close to sober for performances and Fenway is a small circus any way. (I guess I did hear almost every word in spite of staring!) So it was not his leg he drank for, I learned.

Hazel Thatcher told me all these things without a single cruel word and I do admire her for that, not tearing at her husband who could not defend himself but being thoughtful of the reason for his weakness.

I would not say more if I was telling this to some one but this is my own Record Book and no one will ever read it being my private concern. So I continue and reveal that Hazel Thatcher (I feel dumb to call her full name as things are) asked me if I cared to have a "jot" of whiskey in my coffee which I said I would not mind. We talked and talked (I do not remember much of that, mostly she asked questions, where I came from, what I had done, what I planned to do) and it was not too long before she added coffee to our whiskey, then forgot the coffee all together.

By then, my head was numb, the wagon seemed to move some under me and, in the lantern light, I thought Hazel the most matchless woman in the world and told her so.

I remember she was holding both my hands on the table, tears in her eyes. "Oh, Clay, it is so hard to be without a man because my husband only cares for drink," she said.

"I'm sorry, I am sorry," I told her.

She drew my hands closer to her self, it was a small table so I could lean further. "I am so lonely all the time," she said, tears rolling down her cheeks.

"Oh, I am sorry," I said. I wanted to say I would take care of her but even roostered as I was, I knew my self to be a clean up man in a saloon and no more.

"Thank you, my dear," Hazel said. She lifted my right hand to her lips and kissed it. Then she kissed my left hand. Then she leaned forward at me. "Please," she whispered.

What I was feeling at that time! I bent forward and her warm, red lips pressed to mine, I tasted her breath, then again and harder; I have never had a girl (woman) kiss like that.

I jumped a little as she pulled back, pushing up the table where I saw she hooked it up, then, with a sigh, fell against me and held my arms and we were kissing fierce, my arms around her and her lips came apart and—Oh, I must pause!

All right, to the finish. (I will burn this Record Book before a human soul shall read it!) We kissed and kissed and Hazel drew down her costume so her b——s were bared, all white and heavy and, before I knew it, we were on her bunk, both n——d as our days of birth. G———in Heaven, she is such a gorgeous female and her body is—well, private Record Book or not, I can not put it down what happened. All I will say is I lost my head and every thing and did not even care her husband was asleep and snoring only several feet away from us, the wagon rattling, rocking as we—did not even *care*!

I remained with her until the middle of the night and four times "claimed" her; or did she claim me? She is some fiery person, those two girls in The Golden Temple seem like dull goats. To be honest, it was the first time I could think of Mary

Jane and not feel bad because I know she could not give me any thing what Hazel did because she is a different sort; I will not go into fine points but I *will* say Hazel—

(*Here I must omit three paragraphs which, in their vivid clinical description, are unsuitable for the general reader. F.L.*)

I returned to my room at nearly five o'clock and slept like two men in a grave yard. Now it is past one o'clock, afternoon, I have to go to work soon but must write down what I remember.

I suppose she is much older than me but I love her. I love Hazel Thatcher and can not wait 'til I see her again!

Later: same day. It appears that many things can happen at the same time.

When I went to work tonight it was to find the *Red Dog* burning. Jim was across the street, watching it so I walked over to him to ask what happened.

Much to my surprise, he told me he had set the fire him self! He said the owner of the *Red Dog* (Mr. German, I have not met) played poker with him last night and lost a pile but did not care to pay it honest there fore hired some trail bum to bushwhack Jim. The trail bum was stupid, missed, and Jim "took care" of him, then went to the saloon, threw down oil lamps, setting them ablaze. He said he would shoot Mr. German like the cur he is (if he could find him) but it would likely bring on wrath from Hickok who is paid by men like Mr. German so he set the saloon on fire instead.

I asked Jim what he meant to do now for employment. He replied he planned "returning to an earlier pursuit"—stage coach driving, said if I am half the rifle shot as I have told him (clearly he does not believe it) I could hire out as guard.

I might do it but for Hazel. I would rather have a job so I can stay nearby her. I admit the idea does appeal to me— being guard, I mean. But Hazel first and fore most.

August 12, 1866

What did I write the other day? Let me look. That many things can happen at the same time. What I meant—a person's life goes on and on the same and then, no warning, every thing is changed.

Now another. I went to the circus to see Hazel, took a while to get her to my self because of Carl, he was not very drunk tonight. I told her about the coach guard job and said I did not mean to take it for I wanted to be with her, asked her to find out if there was some job I could do with the circus so we could be together when ever Carl is drunk or may be she might think to leave him some time if it worked out, her and me.

We were out behind the tents and Hazel was so quiet I wondered what was wrong and asked. I heard a sound of her swallowing in her throat, that is how still it was. Finally, she drew a long breath in and said, "I can not let you do that, Clay."

I failed to know what she was meaning.

"Don't you see how painful it would be for me to have you around when I am married to Carl?" she said.

I began to say again about her may be leaving Carl but she pressed hard against me, hugging me. "Oh, no, my darling," she declared. "You have your own life to lead."

I tried to answer but she went on. "You are much too bright to waste your life being a circus roust about," she said.

"I don't mind," I told her. "It will be—"

"No, no." She shook her head, then kissed me on the lips. "I can not permit it. You have a full life ahead of you."

"But, Hazel—"

"Please, my darling, no," she said.

"But I love you," I told her. "I want to be—"

"And *I* love *you*," she said, "with all my heart, Clay. That is why I can not do this to you."

"But—"

"For another thing, I am too old for you," she said.

"No," I said, protesting. "We could—"

She stopped my talking with another kiss. "No, no," she said. "I could not bear to see you looking at me as the months went by and you began to see me as I am."

"As you am?—you *are*?!" I asked; I was so worked up by then I could not speak a proper English.

She held me tight, I held her tight. "Just remember me as one who crossed your path," she said.

"But, Hazel!"

"No, no," she said, and kissed me once more. "Go quickly," she told me. "And do not look back."

She was the one who went quickly, with a sob, into the night. I stood there feeling sick. I wanted to run after her and make her change her mind but I was not able to move, I felt my legs were anvils.

I do not understand. She says she loves me and I love her; isn't that enough? There is an aching in my chest; I wonder if hearts really break. Oh, G———, I feel so miserable! Is poor Hazel in her wagon now, crying? Does her heart ache too? She is doing this for Carl, I know it. She is sacrificing her self for him, so bravely.

I will never be the same again.

September 14, 1866

My hand is shaking as I write this, still weak from what happened but I want to put it down while still fresh in mind.

What did I say a few months back?—several times while writing in this Record Book, it seems. That I wanted excitement? Well, I have got it and double.

In truth, I never thought the like would happen. My writing in this book has been enough to put a reader (if there was one) to dead sleep. First it was exciting to ride the driver's seat with Jim, armed with pistols and my new Winchester (I am glad I got it rather than carrying a shotgun as suggested by some including Jim), but soon the jolting on my backside and eating dust became a pain.

Also nothing happened, I mean *nothing*. We picked up passengers and shipment, carried them from place to place, stayed overnight at road ranches, or long enough for meals, changed teams at relay stations, traveled thirty-five miles about each eight hours and that was it. The closest to excitement came that time I thought a road agent was stopping us and got ready for action to find out it was a cow boy whose horse had stepped into a chuck hole and broke its leg so had to be shot leaving him afoot. That was my excitement since I started in August as noted in this Record Book.

Again, as in the *Red Dog*, if it was not for Jim I would have quit. But I have written endless of his skill and handling as much as eight "ribbons" at once, and skill at cracking the whip so close he can remove a small fly from a horse's ear never touching the ear. Also have written endless of our talks, and how we know each other well, and are good friends so no more of that.

We were talking when it happened, coming down a grade from Black Rock Pass about seven miles from Fort Dodge. As I recollect, we were discussing Hazel. I was telling Jim I had recovered from the pain but still feel Hazel is a fine woman who is sacrificing herself for her husband.

"Yes, I know the kind," Jim said and I could tell he understood.

I noticed then that he was glancing around. "What are you looking for?" I asked.

"Not for. At," he answered.

I looked around but did not see a thing. "At what?" I asked.

"Twenty or so Cheyenne," he answered.

I felt my heart bump at these words and looked around more carefully. I saw some movement in the distance; horses and riders it appeared.

"Did they just show up?" I asked.

"No," Jim told me. "They have been trailing us all afternoon."

I was amazed to hear that, which makes it certain I will never be a stage driver or guard of any value. I felt a fool to hear it but pretended not by asking Jim why the Red Skins did not rush us if they wanted to—they had us beaten in numbers.

"They will probably make their move before we get much closer to the Fort," he said.

His words came true before another fifteen minutes had gone by. I felt myself shiver as the Red Skins started riding in at us, galloping their ponies. I raised my rifle but Jim said wait 'til they were closer which I did.

Soon the Cheyennes—twenty-one—were galloping across our path and moving in a line like a traveling circle which, in time, they started to draw in like a noose around our coach. I raised my Winchester again but Jim said not to waste my powder as the "breech clouts" were still not close enough to us. I thought they were; they were no further than those Secesh soldiers I was able to hit during the War, still it is true these targets were moving more.

"Pass down mail sacks to the people and tell them to barricade them selves," Jim told me. He cracked his whip and the team of six (I wished there were eight) leaned forward in their traces, moving faster.

I put my rifle in its boot and started handing down the mail sacks to the four passengers, telling them—as Jim told me—to look to what ever weapons they might have as it was likely they were going to have to defend them selves.

Before forgetting, I must put down that, though this was the first time I have been in mortal danger since the War (the event with Menlo happened too fast for me to feel anything), the emotion I had in those long ago days came rushing back full force—no fear what ever; I felt keyed up and anxious for the battle to commence. It is only now I see how dangerous it was and find it strange I did not feel it as such.

Then I was all pitched up for the fighting. I remember shouting at those Red Skins as they rode in their moving circle, getting closer and closer. "Come on, you b——s!" I yelled. "We are ready for you!"

Finally, they did—with a series of blood-curdling "whoops"—and the battle was on! "*Now* start firing!" Jim shouted. "And show me how good you are!"

It was a fierce battle because those Red Skins do know how to ride and they can duck while riding which makes shooting at them not an easy task. They also shoot not bad for savages; I wonder where they got their rifles and who taught them.

Jim drove the coach as fast as the team could pull it, cracking his whip across their heads so that it sounded like the firing of a pistol. The coach creaked awful as we sped; there was a woman passenger inside who screamed in fright. The rocking and skidding did not help my shooting either, nor the shooting of the passengers; I do not believe their firing hit a single Red Skin.

So it was up to me and I must say I did all right! I kept on firing at those Cheyennes and that Winchester is some good weapon! No matter how those Indians galloped or dipped or ducked, I kept on hitting them one by one; I think it all took place in only minutes too, though noisy minutes what with the thunder of the hooves, and wheels creaking, and the woman screaming, shots and howling Savages, it was a scene straight out of H————! Yet even so I gave seven of the Red Skins one-way tickets to their Happy Hunting Ground, finally—I believe—impressing Jim with what I told him I could do but he had never seen me do. For he yelled and whooped him self and even laughed once which I hardly ever hear him do.

The last Cheyenne I got appeared to have a charmed life for he kept on riding at us with a lance to throw. I kept missing and the woman in the coach was screaming out of her mind before the Red Skin was only ten feet or so away and I was able to shoot him off his horse. He went tumbling and another Cheyenne pony trampled on him. After that, the Indians slowed down and gave up; may be he was Chief or some thing though he had no Head Dress on.

Speaking of charmed lives, mine held up; well, almost. In the War, despite the Minnie balls around me and many explosions, I was not touched. This time, with only twenty-one Red Skins, I took an arrow in my right leg underneath the knee which is odd because I never felt it 'til the Cheyenne left us be. By then, how ever, I had lost some lot of blood (my boot was full of it) and things began to swim around me so I almost toppled from the seat to my death, I am sure, under heavy wheels. Jim grabbed me by the belt and held me from falling while he drove. That is one I owe him as he no doubt saved my life.

He also may have saved my leg (the Doctor said) for, when the Indians had moved off, Jim stopped the coach to bind my leg and "cauterize" the place the arrow went in. He broke off the back part of the arrow, pulled it out, then opened a bullet and poured its powder into the wound. It is lucky for me I was almost "out" any way for if I knew what he was going to do I would have given him a fight. Because when he set fire to the powder, I had a pain as I have never known in all my life, and screamed just like that woman (I am not ashamed to tell it), and passed out cold. Jim put me in the coach, my leg wrapped with his bandanna and drove me to the Fort where now I am.

I am writing this from bed. The Doctor says my wound is not too serious but I will be "out of action" for a while.

September 19, 1866

Jim came in to see me, brought some candy and a news paper to read. There is a little story in it of the "Indian Attack On Stage" and how a "Mr. Cley Halsem" shot some of the "pursuing Savages" to help "save the day." Give credit to that Cley Halsem, he is one fine shot, who ever he is.

Jim said the company has replaced me as guard on his run which does not please me but he said he talked them into giving me a post as helper at the Blue Creek Way Station. The work will not be hard, they told Jim, odds and ends, and when I have recovered from my leg wound I will get back my job as guard, I hope with Jim again; he says he will request it.

I start at Blue Creek next Monday so guess all is well for now.

Little did Clay know. F.L.

October 8, 1866

Another rotten day. Leg hurts like H————. Zandt knows I have been hit there by an arrow but does not seem to care a D————, has me on my feet constant, day and night. He woke me up last night after sleeping only two hours, said a coal oil lamp exploded in the Station house, wanted me to clean the mess. I tried to tell him I was tired having worked since six o'clock yesterday morning but he shoved me hard and said, "I vant it *now*, vare stayin?—(what ever that means) so had to rise to do it. He is a real b————d for certain.

October 10, 1866

I swear he did it on purpose, knocked that deck of cards all over the floor just to make me pick them up.

October 11, 1866

He yelled at me in front of all those people because some one had knocked the soap on the dirt instead of putting it on the dish outside as if it was my fault. I know he did it to "show off" in front of two lady passengers to make them think how big a man he is. I hate him.

October 13, 1866

I think my leg is getting worse. I limp more now than when I came and it aches some thing fierce, some times bleeds a little, cracking open. You think that means a d———to Zandt? "Vat are you, *cripple*, Halzer? *Move!*"—and shoves me on the back.

Lying here, never more "washed out" in all my days. A spider crawling on my leg, I am too tired to brush it off.

October 14, 1866

Heard today, from a passing driver, that, before I came, there was a Mexican named Juan who was helper. Zandt made his life so miserable he took off one night without pay or belongings, never has been seen again. I can understand. I would leave my self but my leg is hurting terrible and I could not walk. I would not steal a horse, that is too dangerous out here, better kill a man than steal a horse. I do not have enough dinero to buy a stage ride out allowing Zandt would let me go. So what can I do?

He rags me some thing awful. Mother was a angel compared.

He limps like I do but worse when I am around with people watching. If it was not for my d——d wound I would go at him full tilt. The way it is, I will be lucky if he does not ruin my leg for life.

I can not go regardless but if I could I do not think I would; that would be running from him and I will never do that from a bully.

Oh, the H———.

October 16, 1866

Too tired to write. Zandt has been at me all day. I have been working like a mule since five o'clock this morning, now is past eleven at night. I must *sleep*.

October 17, 1866

Some thing new, worse. I am ready to do some thing *hard* in return, I swear I am. Leg aches like a tooth ache but I can not pull it out like a tooth can be.

Today, when the afternoon run from Leonardville came by, Zandt grabbed me in front of every body and wrestled me, threw me on the floor. I landed on my left elbow which is swelling and now also aches. D——— him any way! I wish I could pump lead into him like I did those Cheyennes! He is too big to fist fight. G——— d———, he is a son of a b———!

October 19, 1866

I do not know how much more I can stand. I feel close to murder. Zandt is the worst bully I have known in my life. Menlo was a comrade compared. Zandt does all these things:

1. He over works me.
2. He under feeds me.

3. He makes fun of my limp.
4. If I feel sick or weak, he mocks me.
5. He shoves me around and hits me on the back a lot.
6. He rags me in front of passengers and wrestles me, knowing I am too weak to resist.
7. How to say this? There is some thing "odd" about him. When he is not ragging me or bullying and has a few drinks "under his belt," he puts an arm around me, hugs me like a girl and says I am "a good-looking young fellow." Once touched me in a certain spot.

I made it certain I will not stand for this. That only makes him wrathy and he throws me around some more. Today he flung me down so hard my leg wound cracked again and blood leaked out.

I am getting close to some thing and do not like what I feel close to. I will not run off no matter what, like some cur with my tail between my legs. Yet I am not strong enough to give him back his own "brand" of medicine.

Some thing has to break.

What Clay could not have known, which I have now established, is that Emil Zandt had been an officer in the Prussian Army and been dishonorably discharged for attempting "liaisons" with certain of the more youthful men in his command.

Additionally, it should be noted (since Clay does not), that Zandt was a giant of a man, some six feet four or five inches in height and weighing in excess of two hundred and fifty pounds. As stated earlier, Clay Halser was no taller than five feet ten and, at the time, because of his hampered convalescence, weighed at least a hundred pounds less than the hulking German.

Lastly, it is noteworthy to observe that Clay rejected the notion of retreat; typical of him. In retrospect, it seems that, surely, there was some way he might have backed off from the situation. As it turned out, although his consequent action is understandable (if not justifiable), it forged yet one more

*heavy link in the chain which was, one day, to hold him fast in
its tangled length.*

October 23, 1866

It is ended and I am not sorry. If I fry in H——— for it, I will
not say that I am sorry for what happened.

It started as the night stage from Stockdale came in so the
passengers could warm them selves and eat some food. It was
bitter cold with whistling wind and people came in quickly,
stood before the crackling fire and warmed their bodies while
I helped prepare the food and drink.

As always, Zandt began to "put on" for the passengers, the
women mostly (there were two), showing them how he could
rag me as he chose. He had been drinking all the day and put
his hand on me once, which I knocked off so his face got red
with anger; he was in a black mood.

He was never worse, pretending to the passengers he was a
rogue and full of fun instead of the b———d he was. He kept
punching my arm and slapping me on the back, knocking me
off balance, being "jovial" as he said.

When every one was eating, he began to wrestle me and
hold me tight to make me look the fool I was, so helpless in
his arms. His face was red and white in patches, and his
whiskey breath steamed on my face, and made me sick.

I got so mad I twisted hard and was able to break free which
surprised him, I believe; he did not realize I was some stronger
in spite of little sleep and food.

"*Zo,*" he said. "You are ze little *worm* tonight." He laughed
to show the people he was playing at a game but I knew he
was not playing, not from the look in his red pig eyes, like
Menlo. I had never noticed 'til then.

He moved at me and I backed off. "*Zo,*" he said. "You
think you can outvit me."

He reached for me but I slapped his big, fat hand aside.
This made him frothy that I gave him back so much because
it hurt his pride; he did not like to have me giving back what

he liked "dishing out." He kept moving at me and I told him leave off, I did not want any more.

That made him crazy, I believe, to hear me talking up in front of all those people, mostly the women. He lunged at me and I dodged side ways, knowing if he caught me he would do his best to hurt me and could squeeze so hard with me in his arms he might crack my ribs.

"Oh, leave the young man alone," one of the women said.

That got all Zandt's bristles up for sure. He did not pretend he was all jovial now. He looked as mean as he was feeling and that was much. He began to stalk me around the room, ignoring any one who said to stop.

He jumped at me, I side stepped but he stuck his leg out so I tripped. I fell down on my right leg and the pain was like the arrow sticking in there when it happened and the powder being burned there. I cried out and he laughed at that. "Vot's the matter, little boy, *hurt* your self?" he said.

I pushed to my feet and he stepped in, started pushing me around, jostling me, and slapping me across the shoulders, "straight arming" my chest, and knocking me backward 'till I hit the wall. By then the pain in my leg was crazing me and, as he stopped in front of me, I made a fist of my right hand and hit him in the face as hard as I could.

That broke the dam. Jumping at me with a curse, he started squeezing me so hard I could not breathe and knew I would pass out. There was nothing I could do, so had to jerk my knee up at his ——— and hit him there as hard as possible. He cried out, backing off, and clutching there in spite of ladies watching. "Zon of a b———," he muttered, "zon of a b———."

He leaped at me but I jumped to the side and he fell on his knees, slipping. The pain of that was too much for him and he bellowed like a bull. Staggering up, he turned away from me, at first to my surprise, then cold dismay as I saw where he headed—to the counter where he kept his horse whip underneath.

Snatching it up, he shook it loose, glaring at me with his pig eyes, breathing heavy.

"Put that away," the stage coach driver said. "There are passengers here."

Zandt gave no attention to him, his eyes intent on me. I started easing toward the door but he was shrewd and cut me off, a mad smile on his lips. *"Zo,"* he said. "You want to *run?"*

I knew he had me and I wondered what to do. I can not say I was afraid but knew that he could cut me to shreds with that whip of his.

The stage coach driver moved at him. "Zandt, *stop* this," he declared.

The next instant, Zandt had brushed him aside like a child and the driver was flying across the room to almost crash into the fire place.

"Now, *girl man,"* Zandt said, and began to flick the whip as he stalked me like his prey.

I did not say one word, knowing it was useless. I kept my eyes on him as he came nearer.

"Now I crack your crust, you little scum," he said.

The whip end shot out, snapping like a pistol shot near my face.

"Stop it!" cried a woman which made Zandt the madder; now his face was closer to purple than red.

He started cracking out the whip end harder, snapping it closer and closer. I tried to grab it but it only tore a chunk of skin from my palm. The passengers were all up from the table now and backed against the wall, several calling for Zandt to stop which he would never do at that point.

Suddenly, the whip end lashed across my neck and I felt fiery pain.

"Got you, girl man!" Zandt cried; I never saw a look so wild, not even on the faces of those Cheyennes.

The whip end snapped again and tore a piece of shirt arm off me and the skin beneath. Fury made *me* crazy now and I began to hurl things at him, dishes, candle holders, fire irons, stools, any thing I could lay hands on. Some hit him, making him more angry yet. The whip cracked faster and faster, tearing at my clothes and body so it felt like slashes of a red hot poker on my flesh.

When the whip end caught me on the cheek and gouged out skin, I lost my mind, it made my right eye hurt so much. With a cry that sounded like some wounded animal, I raced across the room and dived across the counter. Scrambling down some feet, I reared up quick and grabbed the shotgun off the wall. Zandt thought me still where I had disappeared behind the counter and he cracked his whip there, ripping out a piece of log wall.

He was turning to me when I fired both barrels to hit him straight on in the chest and stomach so he fell back with the cry of some dumb brute and, I believe, was dead before he landed.

In the deathly stillness following, all the people stared at me. I did not say a word. I felt a little sick but I was glad that Zandt was dead and still am glad. I put down the empty shotgun and poured my self a drink of whiskey though my hand was shaking so much I could hardly manage.

I regret the need to kill another man who did not have a weapon—unless one thinks the whip such. But there was nothing else I could do, I had to save my self, he would have blinded and crippled me. Every one in that room said I had a right to defend my self so I do not feel worried over that. I will surrender myself to the hands of the law and feel certain of a fair trial under the conditions of what truly happened.

November 19, 1866

I have not been "up" to writing several days. It is not my Record Book was taken; I have kept it hidden under my shirt. No, the reason I have not been able to write is I am so shocked by what has happened all I did was sit and stare in dumb amazement at the wall.

I am to hang.

Hang.

I can not believe it even now that I have put the words in my own hand. I sat in my cell day by day waiting for the judge to come so my trial would take place. No one (certainly not me) believed I was in danger. Even the Marshal—a man named Dolan who is kind to me—believed the trial would be short and in my favor.

No.

The trial was short all right but not in my favor. I had no defense, it turned out. Not one of the passengers or driver or guard who saw what happened at Blue Creek that night were any where near, so all the judge could see was that I shot a "Unarmed" man with a double shotgun charge; so I was guilty— murder—now to hang.

Hang!

I am still in a daze about it. My head feels numb, my stomach seems empty like hollowed out. In less than two weeks, the hang man will be here and I will drop, my neck will—J——s! It is not fair! I did not murder Zandt! If I had not shot him, he would have whipped me clear to death! That is no guess but certain! I am not the kind to kill a man in cold blood! I am *not*! I shot those soldiers in a War, I made Menlo shoot him self by accident (in self defense) and that is *it*! No murders. None. I was defending my self. *Defending* my self!

Oh, to H———— with it! To G———— d———— H————
with every body!

November 21, 1866

I have got a cell mate, a Texan near my age. His name is
Henry Blackstone and he told me he has been "in jug" a lot of
times. He was found guilty of robbing a store and murdering
the clerk which he claims he did not do for the good reason
he robs only stage coaches.

He also seems entertained by my anger. He says he has no
bad feelings against me but finds my "distress an amusement" because I believed I would get a fair trial.

I was reading about the trial in the *Riverville Clarion* today, raging at the lies and half lies in the story. To read it, you
would think I was a heartless brute who decided it would be a
good joke to kill Zandt. Finally, I flung the paper off from me
but Blackstone only smiled, lying on his bunk. "Do you really
expect to find the truth in a news paper?" he asked. He shook
his head. "You never will, old fellow." That is what he calls me.

He seems so calm and easy going about every thing, it is
hard to believe he is, also, sentenced to hang.

November 24, 1866

I talked with Henry today; he says to write in my Record
Book to say Hello. To *who*?

Any way, he says we have no chance of beating the hang
man's noose so might as well "accept our fate." He says that
young men like us never have a chance because the world is
against us. I never thought of it before but, when you think
about what brought me here, it was not justice, that is sure.
Coming west because of Menlo is another thing. Henry says
it was a "bad break" as in a game of pool, nothing more. We

are the kind of people who get bad breaks all the time, he says; that is just the way it is and nothing we can do about it. Even G——— does not care what happens to people like us.

I hate to believe that but what else can I do? It seems to make sense when you think what has happened to me. The only thing left is to die "without a murmur" Henry says; show the dirty b——s we will not crack in front of them.

I think I would rather try to break free on the day they mean to hang me, force them to shoot me down so death comes fast.

November 25, 1866

No, I will not die without a murmur! I am going to scream out curses at the b——s! I will tell them what I think about their G——— d——— d justice!

November 26, 1866

Henry and I talked today of cutting our arms some how and cheating the hang man and "justice" but decided it was better to let them see how brave men can die.

November 27, 1866

I have decided not to make a sound, just stand there glaring at every body, showing how low I think they are.

But there is the hood. How can I glare at them . . . ?

November 28, 1866

I intend to *scream* at them, the stinking b——s!

November 29, 1866

One of the prisoners is sick (a Mexican) and there is fear that he has come down with small pox. There is a panic rushing through the town; we see them in the street talking of it. A small pox "epidemic" (Henry's word) could wipe out the town. It would not be the first time such has happened.

I hope it does. That is what *I* would call justice. Let the whole d———— town go with us!

November 30, 1866

I could not believe my ears when Henry offered to take care of the sick prisoner. He told the Deputy his father was a doctor so he knows what to do. The Deputy has gone to ask Dolan if it is all right. The Mexican's cell is a mess, smells awful.

I suppose Henry feels if he is going to "swing" any way, he might as well die by small pox as by "strangulation" (another of his words). I think I would prefer the rope as faster.

"I thought you said your father was a cow boy," I asked him a few seconds ago.

"I did," he answered, smiling.

He is very odd.

Later. Still feel dizzy from the speed of it. I feel I may wake up and find it is a dream. I have had dreams like it every night lately which is why it seems unreal.

It went like this. The Deputy came back to say that Dolan had accepted Henry's "generous" offer. Henry said (to me) he knew they would ahead of time because it would give them some chance to "isolate" the disease, as he said, where if they had to go near the Mexican them selves or leave his cell un-cleaned, the small pox might spread.

The Deputy took out his gun and pointed it at Henry as he unlocked the cell door. Henry smiled and held his hands up in the air, saying, "I am not going to try to escape."

"I know you are not," the Deputy replied.

He took Henry to the Mexican's cell and unlocked the door. Henry went inside the cell and leaned across the Mexican who was lying on the bottom bunk. The Deputy remained in the door way of the cell, gun in hand.

Henry put his palm on the Mexican's brow and felt the skin. He made a humming noise and shook his head. He put his fingers on the man's neck and prodded. Then he whistled softly and looked around at the Deputy. "Yes, it is small pox all right," he said.

The Deputy got a look of dread and took a step back, lowering his gun.

The next instant, he was knocked back by the wooden slopbucket which Henry had, some how, got hold of and hurled through the door way. The Deputy cried out in surprise (and, I must add, disgust) and lost his balance, falling against the cell door on the other side.

Before he could recover, Henry leaped across the space between them like a panther; I have never seen a person move so fast who never seemed to want to move at all. Snatching up the fallen gun, he laid the barrel sharp across the Deputy's skull and knocked him senseless.

He took one breath, then grabbed the Deputy's keys, and ran back to our cell. He unlocked the door and flung it open, grinning at me. "Time to make tracks, old fellow," he said.

I admit to being so surprised by what happened I could not move, staring at Henry.

"You want to *hang*?" he asked.

He did not have to say another word. Pulling on my boots, I shoved the Record Book under my shirt and left the cell. We ran to the Marshal's office where, as luck would have it (for Dolan, Henry said), he was out at lunch. We each took a rifle, Henry a Sharps, me a Winchester, I pushed a Colt under the waist of my trousers and we went outside, Henry wearing the Deputy's jacket, me a blanket wrapped around me for the cold.

There was a horse tied up down the walk and we took it, riding double out of town. I find it a joke now that I hesitated about stealing it, thinking it is bad to steal a horse out here. Then I realized I was supposed to "dangle" any way and could not be hanged twice, so rode the horse without another thought. By fortune (and the cold) no one much was outside in the street and we rode from town without a hitch, trotting the horse first, then galloping when we were out of town.

It was a strange feeling to be free and a wanted man at the same time. Still, the joy of having clean air (even icy cold) in my lungs and being in the open weighed over the bad. I had to laugh and seeing how my breath steamed like a kettle made me laugh harder. Henry asked me what was funny and I told him after all the trouble he went to getting us out, we might both die of small pox any way.

"He does not have small pox," Henry told me.

"But I heard you say . . ."

"That was to trick the Deputy and turn him off from what I was planning," Henry said.

"Then what *does* the Mexican have?" I asked.

"Chicken pox," Henry answered. "People always get the two mixed up."

"How do you know that?" I asked.

Henry smiled and told me that he rode once with a doctor who told him all about it. "Before I robbed him, of course," Henry said.

May be it was not that funny but it struck me so and made me laugh until tears ran down my face.

Then I asked him how he could know it was chicken pox all the way from our cell. He said he couldn't. "That is the risk I took to get a chance at breaking out," he told me.

That sobered me so I asked him what if it *had* been small pox.

Henry smiled. "Old fellow, that is the game we play," he said. "You never know what card you will draw."

I write this in a hut we came across, thank G———because it is so cold outside. Henry is asleep. (He smiles in his sleep.) He says we might as well team up a while as both of us are "fugitives" from the sentence of hanging. I can not see a better idea. He saved my life so I owe him some thing in return.

Besides, he seems a steady person all in all.
One of the more ironic statements in the journal. F.L.

So began a new phase in the life of Clay Halser, his period of adventuring with Henry Blackstone.

Blackstone was a strange, young man, a unique product of his times. On the face of things, he seemed as lighthearted a person as Clay had ever known. According to Clay's entries during this time, Henry Blackstone smiled almost constantly. (As noted, Clay even saw him smiling in his sleep.) Nothing seemed to bother him. Yet something festered underneath. The War and his background scarred him in some way Clay was never to truly comprehend. Behind the beaming countenance and pleasantries, there lurked a violent amorality.

Clay was witness to this in the first community they reached, and it is an interesting insight into his sense of values that he would not condemn Blackstone's action, even though he clearly disapproved of it.

December 8, 1866

Henry killed a man today. I do not know what to make of it. He saved my life and he is certainly good company. Still, I feel uneasy in his presence.

Here is how it happened.

We reached this town at two o'clock in the afternoon.

It was terribly cold (still is!) and we were glad to reach some shelter. The town is called Miller's Fork and I guess it is in Kansas although we have ridden far enough South to be in the Nations, I believe.

We had some money Henry had taken from the Marshal's office when we escaped and we went to have a bath and get our clothes washed. We had a nice sleep in a warm bed, then a hearty supper of steak and eggs, then a few drinks at a saloon. Henry said that all our needs were now accounted for except for one and suggested that we make our way to the nearest w——— house for an evening of "dalliance," as he called it. I agreed and we asked the bar tender where to find one. He told us and, after one more glass of whiskey, we headed in that direction.

It was our misfortune—actually, it was the man's misfortune—to run into a huge man coming out of the w——— house as we were going in. He reminded me of that b——— Zandt because he was so big and ugly in his manner.

"Well, what have we here?" he said. "Don't tell me you two boys are going *inside* this place?" He blocked our way and looked amused.

Henry only smiled and asked him if he would kindly get out of the way.

"I don't think that two young boys like you should go in *here*," the man said, laughing. "I am going to tell your Sunday School teacher you are sneaking off to 'cat cribs' when her back is turned."

"Get out of our way, please," Henry told him.

"Oh, no. You are too young."

Those were the last words the man ever spoke in this world. I did not notice Henry drawing. The first I knew, a shot was roaring in my ears and the big man was falling on the ground with lead in his chest. He twitched once and was dead.

Henry looked at me with a smile. "Let's go in and find some women now," he said. He did not seem concerned about the man.

I thought we should run for it but Henry gave three dollars to one of the w———s and she told the town Marshal that the man had drawn on Henry first and Henry had killed him in self-defense. Which may be the case, I suppose, in fairness to Henry. His eyes may be quicker than mine and maybe that man was just about to go for his gun.

We stayed at the w——— house for the evening but I did not enjoy it much because the killing had disturbed me some. It seems to me that Henry shot that man without a thought and never gave a hint that he intended doing so. I owe Henry my life, that is certain. Still, I am a little restless about his way of thinking.

Later: I asked Henry before he went to sleep why he had killed that man. I was not easy about asking but had to know.

Henry was not disturbed by the question. "I asked him to get out of the way and he wouldn't," he answered.

He explained to me that he can be so cheerful all the time because he never lets anger stew inside him. He told me that, if he had been Zandt's helper, he would have shot him the first day, in the back or in the front.

"Never bear a grudge, old fellow," he told me. "If a stranger starts to rile you, kill him right away. That way you get it 'out of your blood' so to speak and are not poisoned. I am not talking about friends, of course."

I was glad to hear that as I guess (I hope) I am a friend of his.

The entries in Clay's journal through the winter and into the spring of 1867 are cut from the same cloth. Constantly in Henry Blackstone's company, he began to manifest that infirmity of character which had turned him toward indolent pursuits instead of honest labor following the War. He never worked, drank a good deal, learned to play cards almost like a professional and generally caroused through the Indian Nations, Texas, and New Mexico. When things were lean, he was not above a crack at highway robbery, on at least two occasions assisting Henry Blackstone in stagecoach holdups.

None of this is stated as condemnation for he, later, more than compensated for these youthful digressions from the law. It is merely noted to "flesh out" the picture of the young man he was at that point—becoming fully acclimated to the Western mode of life but yet to earn—or be given the chance to earn—the opportunity to prove himself a law-abiding citizen.

An illustrative entry follows.

February 22, 1867

Almost "bought it" tonight. The two of us have never been in such a tight before. How we got out of it, the Lord alone knows.

We were playing poker with some Mexicans on the outskirts of town. I don't even know the name of it except to say we are in Texas.

Henry and I were winning like there was to be no end to it. It was after midnight when he and I began to realize (we think alike, it seems) that, short of some miracle, those Mexicans were not going to let us leave the game except with empty pockets and slit throats.

It was not a cheerful situation to be in, a sod hut on the high ground near a muddy river with the only light a candle on the table and our only "companions" five Mexican b——s who would steal pennies off their Mothers' dead eyes.

Henry moved first. Fortunately, I know how he does things now so when he yawned and stretched, I felt my muscles snap to, ready for the play.

It came fast. Shooting out his hand, Henry doused the candle flame and flung himself to one side of his chair. I did the same. The dark hut was a scene of shouts and curses. Fiery gun explosions followed and I felt the hot wind of lead around me. Henry dove through the window opening a second before I did.

It was good luck for us that the moon was not in sight but bad luck that some s—— of a b—— had taken our horses while we were playing cards.

"The river!" Henry said and we legged it down that slope as fast as we could.

By then, those Mexicans were out the door and shooting after us. I discovered later, to my surprise, that those were the first shots they had gotten off. The shots inside were snapped off by Henry, trying to kill a few of them before we lit out. When I told him that the slugs almost got me instead, he laughed and reminded me that a miss is as good as a mile.

We reached the river bank a few yards ahead of the Mexicans and plunged into the current which was COLD!! I pulled out my revolver and fired off a few shots at the Mexicans but it was too dark and the river current very fast. I held my gun so I wouldn't lose it and we fought our way to shore a distance down the bank, it might have been a half mile.

We found ourselves near the town and ran toward it to steal some horses to replace our own. Our clothes got stiff before we reached it and we moved like wooden creatures held by strings. Then, when we were cutting out two horses from the first house, a pack of hounds came at us. They tore at us insanely, ripping open our clothes and skins. The seat of my trousers was torn out and my rump bit hard. Henry shot one of the dogs and we got on the horses and rode, not bothering to look for saddles.

That was the most agonizing ride in the history of my life! My behind was bare and bloody, freezing cold and pounded to a pulp on that horse's bony back. I think I picked a nag that had not seen a square meal for a month or else was ninety years of age for I felt every bone it had.

As if that was not enough, the Mexicans caught sight of us and took out in pursuit. They would have caught us too if a storm had not come up.

Lightning crashed and I saw clouds like black mountains in the sky. Thunder began and then more lightning. A tornado of wind commenced that not only almost blew us off our horses' backs but almost blew our horses over as well. Finally, hailstones as big as peaches started pounding us before it started raining so hard that it was like riding underneath a waterfall. I swear I thought the Lord above was punishing us for the life we were leading.

Henry must have thought the same thing (though not as seriously as me) for he looked up at the sky and shouted, "Well, old fellow, about the only thing you ain't seen fit to hit us with tonight is *boulders*!"

At that moment, we were riding through a draw and several boulders from above started rolling down at us. We barely managed to escape them. I was scared white but Henry laughed as hard as I have ever heard him laugh. He tipped his hat to Heaven. "Called me on that one, didn't you?" he shouted.

We are taking shelter in a cave now, drying out our clothes over a fire. Henry is asleep as I write. I thank the Lord I keep this Record Book on my person now and did not leave it in my saddle bag.

What Clay refers to as a "bad chill" (probably pneumonia) plus complications from his still not completely healed shoulder wound compelled him to slow the frenetic pace of his schedule and take a job on a New Mexican ranch, first as cook's helper, later as a cowhand. Out of friendship, Henry kept him company and the arrangement worked out reasonably well until late September when Henry shot one of the cowhands over a card game in the bunkhouse. Forced to flee, he left the ranch accompanied by Clay who had, by that time, regained his health.

September 22, 1867

I am on the run again with Henry. He killed Ned Woodridge last evening while they were playing poker. He said that I did not have to light out with him as it is his own trouble but I decided that I owe it to him still.

The chase was not too bad. We got away from the cow boys who were led by Baxter. (*The ranch's foreman. F.L.*) We did get a shock as we were riding though. Suddenly, our horses reared back, terrified, as it appeared that we had galloped straight into an Indian witch!

It turned out to be a dead papoose. We had ridden into an Indian burial ground without knowing it. The papoose had been tied to a tree but the fastening had come loose and the body swung to and fro. It was a grisly sight with its face shriveled up and staring at us, looking very strange with all the beads and ornaments attached to it.

We rode another hour or so and came upon the campground

of a group of men, outlaws as it turned out. To my surprise, Henry said hello to their leader Cullen Baker. They have ridden together in the past.

I have heard about this Baker. Everyone says he is a murderous "desperado" but he strikes me much like Henry. He does not seem aware of his renown and is affable. Like Henry, he smiles a good deal.

I do not know what to do now. Henry has declared that he intends to join forces with Bonney and ride with him again. I do not believe that I am up to living that kind of life again. It is exciting, sure enough, but hard to sleep, never knowing when John Law might pick you up. That time in jail, thinking I was going to hang, was enough for me. I do not want to be a cow boy or a cook's helper, that is for sure. Neither do I choose to be "gallow's meat."

September 23, 1867

It seemed today as if it wasn't going to matter whether I decided to ride with Henry or not!

All of us were riding up a hill and I was thinking how to let Henry know that I was going to split up with him when we heard a noise in the distance that sounded like rolling thunder. The difference was it made the earth shake underneath us.

As we reached the top of a hill, we saw what was causing the noise. Hundreds of stampeding buffalo chased by several dozen Comanches. Seeing us, the Red Skins left off chasing buffalo and started after us. Deciding that caution was the better part of valor, we turned tail.

Those Indians rode too well for us, however, and it became clear that a stand would have to be made. Spotting a deserted trench house in the distance, we rode like H——— until we reached it. Leaping off our mounts, we pulled them inside and slammed the door shut just before those Red Skins reached us.

I can not say if they were drunk or crazy or what but those Comanches sure did want our hides for supper! They kicked and hammered at the door and dove in through the window. Only our constant, accurate fire kept the battle on an even keel. There must have been twenty-five to thirty of them and they just kept coming at us like they were determined to kill us to the last man.

Once, in a lull that lasted a few minutes, I heard a bugle call and told the others, with excited pleasure, that the Cavalry had come to save us. They laughed and said it was an Indian doing it who had, likely, stolen the bugle from a dead Cavalry man. "They like to blow bugles," Henry told me. "It fires them up."

I guess it must have for the next attack came right away. It was a mean one. We fired our guns until they were burning hot to touch. Indian bodies were stacked all over. Our horses screamed and bucked, knocking their heads against the roof of the house. There was so much powder smoke that it was hard to see or breathe. The Comanches yelled, and pounded on the door, and jumped in through the window even though it just meant jumping into lead. I must have shot down seven or eight of them. You did not have to have good aim either. You could not miss them.

Finally, they had enough I guess and what was left of them rode off. (Which was a good coincidence as we were down to nine more shots between us.) Two of Baker's men were killed and nineteen Indians, six inside and thirteen around the house. One of our horses was also killed but, I am glad to state, my "charmed life" has reported back for duty as I did not get so much as a scratch.

When we were leaving—Henry riding double with Cullen—I decided that it was as good a time as any to declare myself and told Henry that I had made up my mind to get myself another ranch job. This is not true but I did not want to tell him that his mode of living is not to my taste any more.

He did not take it hard, only smiling and saying, "Sure thing, old fellow. Good luck to you—" as he rode off. I thought our parting would make him a little sadder than that.

I am sad about it. Even though Henry is a strange person,

he had always been a good friend to me and I am sorry I could never repay his favor by saving his life. I do not suppose I will ever have the chance now.

Adios, Amigo! It has been good fun but our paths go off in different ways now.

About a week later, Clay came upon the camp of an old man with a small herd of cattle. The man had been lying in his bedroll for three days and was close to death.

October 2, 1867

I buried the old man today. He did not have much of a chance to live, I think. I took care of him as best as I could and he seemed grateful. He said that I could have his herd of cattle if I would write a letter to his son in Missouri and tell him what had happened. I promised that I would. The old man's name was Gerald Shaner.

Now I am a cow boy once again. I can not seem to get away from it. I hate those long horns like the plague and now I have to nurse a herd of them across the plains. I say "a herd" but there are only twelve of them! I say "I have to nurse" them but, of course, I don't. I could let them wander off to live or die but that would not be smart. I can use the money they will bring me so I am going to drive them to Hickman which is about a hundred and twenty miles southwest of here and hope to sell them. That is my plan.

As indicated earlier—and a leitmotif throughout Clay's account—his plans "gang aft astray." Judging from a percentage viewpoint, one might declare that Clay's plans were altered by outside influences more than not. This fact strengthens my contention that he was, indeed, a "product" of his times, being led with almost preordained inevitability toward his destiny. This is not to say that he did not have a mind of his own or make decisions on his own. Yet, caught up by the violent wave of the period through which he lived, he could do little more than "keep his head up," swimming short distances in various directions even as the wave bore him on toward his appointment with fate.

The next entry of note occurs almost two weeks later as he nears Hickman with his herd of nine cows, two of them having been lost to Indians, one to a pack of wolves.

October 17, 1867

I came up on the camp at sunset yesterday, the men there working for a ranch called The Circle Seven.

Their foreman, a man named Tiner, was affable at first, inviting me to light and have some food. I accepted gladly and counted myself fortunate to have come this way. He told me that Hickman is just a day's ride away and I decided that I was a lucky fellow to have made it.

Then he surprised the H——— out of me by telling me that, since I was new to these parts and a "one-man spread" I only had to pay them ten dollars to move my herd across their range. He told me this was Circle Seven land and strangers were required to pay for its use.

I was angered by this and told him I did not have a one-bit piece to my name. This did not disturb him. He said that I could pay my way across with one of my cows.

"How can you rake me down like that?" I asked him. "You know that I can get more than ten dollars for one of those cows."

He said that he was sorry about that but that, if I wanted, he could have the cow cut in half or thirds and take ten dollars worth of it for payment.

Something about the way he said that riled me good. I got up and mounted. When he told one of his men to cut out a cow, I told him to keep his d———d hands off. He paid no attention to me and sent the man to do what he had ordered.

I suppose I am crazy but I got so mad at this, I saw red. I told that cow boy to stay the H——— away from my herd. He acted as if I wasn't even talking and started after one of my cows. I pulled out my rifle and shot the ground up by his boots.

That did it royal. The next second, lead was flying and I was forced to ride for my life. I tried to drive my herd off on the run but wasn't very far before they caught me and shot my horse out from underneath me. I had to leg it to a pile of rocks and take cover. It was almost dark by then and although I took a shot or two at them, I don't believe I hit a single target.

Now it is morning and my herd is gone and so are all the Circle Seven men as well. I have no horse so it looks like a long walk ahead for me. If I ever run across those cow stealing b———s, I will let air into them so help me G———!

No further entry appears for five days. Clay's walk across the New Mexican prairie must have been an arduous one. Cowboy boots are hardly designed for hiking (he knocked the high heels off the first day so he could move more easily), and Clay, though healthy, was not accustomed to walking great distances. By the time he reached the property of the Arrow-C ranch, his feet were swollen, blistered, and bloody. He was taken into the ranch by one of the cowboys, fed, and put up for the night.

The following day, he met Arthur Courtwright who probably had more to do with what Clay Halser became than any other individual.

October 20, 1867

I have decided to stay at the Arrow-C and work for Mr. Courtwright.

He is about the nicest gentleman I have ever met and I like him a good deal. He is British and has only been in this country for nine months. He is twenty years older than me but we talk the same lingo. He makes a body feel at ease and has charm enough to talk the birds out of the branches. He seems to have taken a shine to me, I am glad to state. I spent most of the day talking to him.

He told me that his family is a "venerable" one. (I think that is the word he used.) He said that they go back in English history and were, at one time, famous, and rich. Now, although the fame in history is still intact, their riches have faded. He took what was left of the money and "came to The New World to recoup the family fortune" as he put it.

A Hickman man—named Charles McConnell—who Mr. Courtwright met in St. Louis convinced him that this area was ideal for his purposes. Taking McConnell's word at face value, Mr. Courtwright came here, bought this ranch and started a supply store with McConnell in Hickman.

Since coming here, however, he has discovered that the "path to wealth" is not to be an easy one. There is a man named Sam Brady who controls the entire range, holding the best springs, streams, water holes, and grazing lands which makes his ranch (The Circle Seven!) the most powerful around.

I asked Mr. Courtwright why the small ranchers did not join forces to break Brady's "strangle hold." He answered that, until he came here, Brady owned the only supply store in Hickman. Either the ranchers went along with him or they got starved out.

Now that Mr. Courtwright and McConnell have a "rival" store, the tide is changing but it is just beginning to change. Most of the small ranchers are buying their supplies from the Courtwright-McConnell store now and Sam Brady is beginning to hurt. Mr. Courtwright fears "a major conflict" some time soon. He hopes to avoid it but doesn't know that it is possible.

I got the feeling that he feels a little doubt about his partner although he never said it in so many words. I don't even *know* McConnell but I feel doubt about him. I mean, why didn't he tell Mr. Courtwright he was sticking his neck on a chopping block by coming here?

I don't know why Mr. Courtwright told me all these things. He said that he could trust me and asked if I would stay and help him. I said I would be glad to do so and would never stand back in a tight place. I would help him even if it was just because he asked, I like him that much.

But for a chance to get back at those Circle Seven b———s, I would take a situation in H———!

What Clay did not realize was that, by taking employ at the Arrow-C he was doing just that; taking a situation in H——.

So he began to work for the Britisher Arthur Courtwright whom he came, quickly, to revere. Clay never mentioned his own father or expressed any sense of loss at never having had a father-son relationship. It seems clear, however, that, in Courtwright—who, by all reports, was a man of infinite charm, patience, and wisdom—Clay found the father he had never had.

He also found, within the month, the young woman he was, consequently, to wed.

November 28, 1867

Mr. Courtwright was kind enough to take me with him today into Hickman where we had Thanksgiving dinner at the home of his partner, Charles McConnell.

I cannot say I like McConnell worth a d——— although I would never say this to Mr. Courtwright if my life depended on it. I think McConnell is not to be trusted. I found out, to my surprise, that he was, at one time, Sam Brady's lawyer! This is not what I would call a good "omen." If a man can turn on one he can turn on another. If he ever proves to be false to Mr. Courtwright's trust, I will kill him.

That would not be so easy to do however. I do not mean as a physical act. (McConnell is a weak tub of a man.) I mean it would not be so easy to do because of his daughter, Anne, who I met today.

I don't trust myself any more where it comes to the heart but I have the feeling that I could fall in love with Anne McConnell very easy. There is something about her that reminds me of Mary Jane Silo. (It is hard to believe that it is getting close to *two years* since I saw her last!) She is very pretty and has a gentle smile that pleases the eye.

I must not let myself be fooled however. I thought I was in love with Hazel Thatcher. What is more, I have had many females since (all w——s) and may not have the ability to feel an honest emotion.

I do feel *something* though—and something powerful. I hope I am not fooling myself to believe that she feels something too. I can not believe, however, that the looks and smiles she gave me were without meaning.

I *do* believe that her father does not care for me. When I was looking at his daughter, I noticed him frowning. I guess he knows that I am only a common ranch hand and wants more for his daughter. Because Mr. Courtwright is his partner though and Mr. Courtwright likes me, McConnell can't say anything right out.

I don't believe that Mrs. McConnell noticed anything of what passed. She is Anne's stepmother and seems very retiring in nature.

Clay's ability at character analysis deserted him on this occasion as a later entry makes vividly clear.

December 14, 1867

God All Mighty, what a strange H——— of an afternoon!

Mr. Courtwright sent me in to Hickman to deliver a message to Mr. McConnell. He was not at home but Mrs. McConnell was.

It is not often that you smell whiskey on a lady's breath. A w——'s yes but not a lady's. I smelled it on Mrs. McConnell's breath however. Her eyes had a faraway look in them and she moved oddly.

I did not know what to say when she told me to come inside the house. I thought, at first, she meant for me to sit and wait until her husband got home so I could deliver the message to him personally. On second thought, that did not make much sense but, by then, I was already in the house.

Mrs. McConnell embarrassed me by offering me a drink

of whiskey. I said no thank you and she had one any way. I sat on the sofa which she told me to do. I tried to be polite and make conversation with her but it was hard.

Too late I remembered Hazel Thatcher and that night in the wagon as Mrs. McConnell put her hand on me. I don't mean on my *hand* either! I was so surprised I must have turned into a statue!

She started saying things to me that I can not put down even if this *is* a secret journal! I mean I never heard such talk from a female, not even a w———! I tried to get up and excuse myself but she wouldn't let me. I know I was blushing because my face felt as though I was holding it a few inches from a red hot stove.

Then she cursed and pulled open her dress and buttons popped all over. She had nothing on underneath and I near to froze when she held her bare b——s in her hands and told me to ———!

I couldn't even speak I was so startled by the turn of events! She was grabbing me and telling me she wanted me to———her right there on the sofa in the full light! I swear to G———, fighting those Comanches was a sight easier than fighting off that woman.

To top it all, Anne came in just then! Seeing her, her stepmother cursed something awful, then ran upstairs and slammed a door. I stood dazed and looking at Anne, believing that she was going to tell me to get out of the house and never come back.

To my surprise, she asked me to sit down. She was blushing too as she sat across the parlor from me and told me that her stepmother is "ill" and that she would honor me if I would not say anything about what had happened as it would break her father's heart. I agreed and, shortly after, left. When I did, she kissed me on the cheek and said that she was grateful to me and hoped that we might see each other again under "more pleasant circumstances."

I take back what I said. I *do* love Anne McConnell. I believe that I must ask for her hand in marriage.

It is going to be d———d awkward though. I mean, for

G——'s sake what am I supposed to say the next time I see her stepmother? It is such a dreadful problem, I can not even ask Mr. Courtwright what *he* would do though I am sure that he would give some good advice.

December 15, 1867

A few lines remaining in this, my first Record Book that I found on the belongings of that Confederate officer more than three years ago.

I am going in to Hickman in a few days to pick up some supplies for Mr. Courtwright. While I am in town, I will buy myself another Record Book.

BOOK TWO

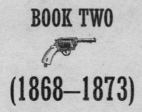

(1868–1873)

If the purpose of this work were to present a story of young love in the West, circa 1867–68, a modest volume in itself would be prepared from this period of Clay's life during which he came to know and love Anne McConnell. Like all young men in any given period of history, Clay rhapsodizes endlessly about his loved one's beauty, and charm, and the total wonderment of their feeling for each other.

Whenever he was not actually working for his employer, Clay was seeing Anne or dreaming of her, filling countless pages in his second Record Book (sixty-eight in all) with youthful outpourings.

As to his "courtship" of Anne McConnell, it consisted, as courtships usually do, of walks and rides together, dances attended, visits at the McConnell house or at the Courtwright ranch. Clay says nothing more of Mrs. McConnell except to note that he almost never saw her after the unsettling incident in the McConnell parlor. Doubtless, she remained to herself whenever there was any possibility that their paths might cross.

Anne's father continued to object to her relationship with Clay but never strongly enough to make a difference—especially when it started to become apparent that Courtwright's feeling for Clay was that of a man for his son which, of course, considerably illuminated Clay's potential as a son-in-law.

All in all, this was a time of happiness for Clay. He had found a home, a father, a bride-to-be, and a potentially stable future. So wrapped up was he in these individual pleasures that he even forgot his animosity toward the Circle Seven ranch, feeling that "fate" had more than compensated him in other ways.

As indicated, however, this is not *a story of young love but a tale of mounting violence in which Clay was to enact a bigger role with each succeeding year.*

Accordingly, we skip, in time, to August of 1868 when Brady made his first clear move to break Courtwright's increasing control of the small ranchers in the area.

August 12, 1868

The "conflict" Mr. Courtwright foresaw when I first met him seems to be beginning.

This afternoon, Sheriff Bollinger came out to the ranch with a warrant for Mr. Courtwright's arrest. It has been obvious to all that Bollinger is Brady's pawn but no one thought he would make it as clear as this.

Bollinger told Mr. Courtwright that Brady was claiming ownership of the Arrow-C. He said that Brady had a paper from the ranch's former owner which signed over the ranch to him in payment for a debt. Mr. Courtwright explained to the Sheriff (I would have chased him off the ranch) that this was "ancient history" as he called it. He said that the former owner had never filed for the land whereas he had. This made Brady's paper "invalid." Bollinger allowed as how that might be true but Courtwright had to come and face trial any way.

I told Mr. Courtwright (taking him aside) that he should not surrender himself to the Brady forces but he said that he had no fear as he was in the legal right and they would not dare to hurt him openly.

I did not like it. There was no reason why this claim on the ranch should be brought up again. I suspected Bollinger and followed him and Mr. Courtwright at a distance.

My suspicion proved a true one. I saw Bollinger draw his revolver and point it at Mr. Courtwright. Later, Mr. Courtwright told me that Bollinger said the warrant was only a ruse. There was to be no trial because he was never to reach Hickman alive. When asked what had happened, Bollinger was going to say that Mr. Courtwright had tried to escape and that he had to shoot him.

He will never say it now, by G——! He will never say another lie to anyone. I grabbed my rifle and aimed as fast as I have ever aimed in my life. Before he could pull the trigger, I blew him off his saddle. It was a lucky shot. I got him the first time.

I rode down to Mr. Courtwright who was very white and shaken. I told him that, from now on, I would not let him put himself in such danger. He did not argue with me. All he kept saying was, "I had no idea they would try a thing like this."

A month later, a second "arresting party" rode out to the Arrow-C, led by Bollinger's brother who had been appointed as the new Sheriff.

September 13, 1868

Brady made himself as clear as day this afternoon.

Mr. Courtwright, Tom (*the foreman of the Arrow-C. F.L.*) and I were having dinner when a group of riders pulled up at the ranch house. Tom and I put on our guns and went outside to see what was going on.

It turned out to be *another* Sheriff Bollinger (the former one's brother has been made the Sheriff) and four of his Deputys. He said that he was here to take in Mr. Courtwright for the murder of his brother.

"You are not taking any one," I told him.

"I will take him a corpse or a living man," he answered.

"Take *me*," I said, "for *I* am the one who shot your brother."

He looked at me in surprise. Later, Tom said that, even though I am twenty-two years old, I look like a boy and this was what set back Bollinger. "*You*?" he said.

"*Me*," I said. "As I will shoot down any s——— of a b——— who tries to murder Mr. Courtwright."

Bollinger started cursing at me but Tom told him to get off

the Arrow-C unless he was prepared to sling lead for the privilege.

Bollinger said no more. He looked at us a while, then pulled his horse around as did his Deputys. Something warned me that he had some other play in mind so I said, low, to Tom, "Pretend to turn away."

We did that and, from the corners of my eyes, I saw Bollinger go for his gun.

"Down!" I cried and threw myself across the porch, snatching out my revolver. Tom ducked behind a porch chair and lead started flying. Tom and I had the advantage being in the shadows of the porch. Tom brought down one of the Deputys, and I killed another, and wounded Bollinger. The group took off at high speed. I am sure they will be back.

Mr. Courtwright had been watching at a window. He told me afterward that he was much impressed by my "instinctive prowess" (his words) with the hand gun. He said that I should practice at it and become "adept" as I am certain to be one of Brady's "principal" targets now.

I have never thought about the hand gun much. I have used it, of course, but never given it consideration as a weapon, preferring the rifle. I can see, however, that there are times when one must defend himself at close quarters and a rifle is useless for that.

I suppose that I had better practice some and try to get a little better.

"I suppose that I had better practice some and try to get a little better."

With these simple words, Clay embarks on his brief career as one of the deadliest gun fighters ever spawned by the frontier. I am certain that he had no conception of his future when he wrote those words. Thinking, no doubt, that he was, merely, developing a skill that would help him to protect his employer, he could not have dreamed of the violent path down which he would be led by this mastery.

A mastery he acquired with almost consummate ease, I would add. Where other men might have had to practice for

*years, Clay became incredibly "adept" in a matter of months.
Possessed of near to preternatural reflexes (eyewitness accounts of his gun battles verify this time and again) and a virtually infallible sense of direction, he discovered that his
ability increased by leaps and bounds as he learned "to start
my lead pump fast."*

*Learn he did, using a five-month period of stalemate be-
tween the Brady-Courtwright forces to refine his natural skill
at drawing and firing accurately at high speed. Although he
learned to do this ambidextrously, he elected—after much
experimentation—to confine himself to the "cross" draw,
wearing his scabbard on the left side, the butt of his revolver
reversed; he preferred, at this time, a Single Action, .41 caliber Colt.*

*That he soon would have use of this newly developed skill
was a fact not lost on Clay as he wrote, during the winter of
1868, "There is going to be powder burned soon."*

March 23, 1869

I am writing this on a piece of brown paper that I took from
the store a while ago. Later on, I will write these words in my
Record Book.

We are under siege. It has been going on since morning.
We are in the grain house out in back of Mr. Courtwright's
store—Mr. Courtwright, McConnell, Benton, Stanbury, Grass,
and myself. All the rest are dead and Mr. Courtwright's store
is nearly burned to the ground. This is the first time I have
had a moment's breath since morning. It is only for a moment
too. We will have to make a break for freedom soon or die.

Bollinger (that b———!) and his men waited until we were
in Hickman. He must have been planning this for months. It
came as a surprise to us since we had been looking for an attack on the ranch.

We were in Mr. Courtwright's store getting supplies when
Bollinger came in and said I had to surrender myself for the
murder of his brother. I refused, naturally. This did not appear

to surprise him. He said that he had done his duty now and whatever happened afterward was on our heads. He left the store and, five minutes later, the firing began.

Bollinger must have had thirty or forty men out there because the lead came flying hot and heavy, breaking all the windows and making Swiss Cheese of the walls. I grabbed Mr. Courtwright and pulled him down behind the counter. He never showed fear. I admire him the more for that. He has behaved with courage all day long which is more than I can say for that sniveling son of a b———, McConnell!

Any way, although we were much outnumbered (there were nine of us to begin with), we kept Bollinger's forces off because of our accurate rifle fire. I got a Winchester Repeater from the rifle cabinet and was able to hit many living targets in the next few hours. Once again, my "charmed life" is in evidence and, although things look grim, I feel full of cheer and am confident that we will get out of here safe and sound.

About four o'clock, we had lost three men and decided to retreat to the grain house which is made of stone as the fire set by Bollinger's men was getting too hot to bear. While we were running, poor Tom took a slug in the back of his head and died in a second. He was a brave man. The rest of us got into the grain house alive although Grass and Benton are wounded, Grass in the right leg, Benton in the left thigh.

It is almost dark now and we are going to have to make a run for it shortly. If we can get to the ranch we will be all right.

Later: We are at the ranch. Mr. Courtwright has a slight wound in his arm but is otherwise untouched. I have no wounds at all.

We broke out after six o'clock. It started raining and the fire started smoking quite a lot. As wind began to blow the smoke across the yard, we ran out, one by one. I was close behind Mr. Courtwright as we dashed across the yard and over the wall. There was a perfect hail of lead but we were untouched except, as I said, for a slight wound to Mr. Courtwright's left arm. Poor Glass was killed however and Stanbury is a prisoner.

So is McConnell but I don't give a d———— about that. He refused to leave the grain house, crying and pleading with us to surrender so the "bloodshed" would stop. Finally, I shoved him in a corner and we took out.

After making the wall and going over it, we ran through the back alleys and found some horses tied up in front of *The Latigo Saloon,* which we quickly "commandeered" and used to ride back to the ranch. Mr. Courtwright says that he will send them back tomorrow, which shows what an honest man he is even at such a time.

I do not know what he is going to do now. The store had more than two-thirds of his money in it and is a total loss. He says that he will not give in to Brady though for which I admire him even more. Still, what is he going to do?

I do not know how I am going to see Anne now as I can not ride into Hickman any more without risking life and limb.

As for her father, I hope they hang the b———— by his——! He is a miserable coward and nothing more.

What Clay did not know at the time was that McConnell, after being captured by Bollinger, was given a choice of helping Brady deal with Courtwright or being killed. Being, as Clay accurately appraised, "a miserable coward and nothing more," he quickly agreed to help Brady in order to preserve his own existence.

March 27, 1869

I am writing this before I leave for Hickman. I may not come back alive but I do not care as long as I get whoever is responsible for Mr. Courtwright's death.

I had been up for two straight days on guard and had fallen asleep in exhaustion. While I was asleep, McConnell rode out to the ranch and told Mr. Courtwright that Brady wanted to parley in town and declare a truce. (Benton told me this.) Mr. Courtwright had been terribly upset since the attack on his store and wanted to believe that what McConnell said was true. Immediately, he had his horse saddled and started into town beside McConnell.

When I woke up and found that Mr. Courtwright was gone, I saddled fast and rode for Hickman, feeling a cold weight in my stomach because I knew, somehow, exactly what had happened.

I found Mr. Courtwright at the bottom of a draw, his body riddled by lead. There were hoofmarks all around the spot and I calculate that four men must have been in on the murder, one of them McConnell.

I brought Mr. Courtwright's body to the house and, I confess, spilled hot tears every foot of the way. I have never known a finer man in my life and say openly that I loved him and respected him as I would love and respect a father. D——— his killers! I will find them if it takes me twenty years! And if I die in getting them, that is all right too.

I am leaving now. G——— help those who murdered Mr. Courtwright for vengeance is riding after them.

Later: I rode to Hickman and went first to the McConnell house. Anne opened the door when I knocked and told me that her father was not there.

I did not believe her and pushed inside. I searched the house from top to bottom and found him hiding in the cellar. He had a Derringer in his hand but did not pull the trigger, knowing that he was a dead man if he did.

I told him that I wanted to know who had been with him when he murdered Mr. Courtwright. I heard Anne gasp when I said that, then she said no more.

McConnell started crying and begging for his life. He swore that he had had no notion that Brady meant to murder Mr. Courtwright. I yelled at him and asked him what in H——— he *did* think Brady meant to do! He could hardly answer me, he was so scared. He swore on his Mother's grave that he had not drawn a gun but had ridden off when he saw the three men waiting to kill Mr. Courtwright.

I asked him who they were but he would not tell me, saying that his life would not be worth a plugged nickel if he told. I put my Colt against his forehead and swore that I would drench the cellar wall with his brains if he did not answer. Anne began to cry and grabbed my arm. I pushed her off and told McConnell again that I would kill him if he did not tell me who the men were.

He answered that the three hired by Brady were not from Hickman. He said that they have been staying at the hotel but he did not know if they were still in town.

I was going to kill him where he stood but Anne was pleading for his life and, despite my fury, I could not make myself kill her father in front of her eyes. I left the house and went to the hotel. The clerk told me that the three men were not checked out but were not in their rooms. I went to the cafe but they were not there either.

I found them in *The Latigo Saloon.* They were standing at the counter, drinking and laughing, bragging about the "Limey" they had "put to rest" that afternoon.

As soon as they said that, I pulled out my gun and pushed in through the bat wing doors, firing and snapping as fast as I could until the gun was empty. They did not expect me and not one of them had time to draw, but I do not feel remorse about murdering them the way they murdered Mr. Courtwright. One of them was wounded, lying on the floor. I reloaded my revolver and stepped over to him, putting a ball between his eyes as he begged for his life. I left the three of them dead and rode back to the ranch.

There is nothing left now but to leave. I can not ask Anne to go with me and doubt that she would if I did ask. I feel numb inside. It is impossible for me to believe that everything has changed so much. A week ago, my life was perfect. Now everything is ended and the world seems black to me.

I will leave in a . . .

Anne just left. She rode out from town to beg me not to leave. She said that she and her father will testify on my behalf. I do not believe that McConnell will do anything of the kind no matter what he told her. I *do* believe Anne though. She said that she will tell the jury at the trial exactly what her father said about Brady making him go out to invite Mr. Courtwright into town for a parley and how the three men were waiting on the trail to murder him instead.

Still, I am not sure. Brady still controls the town. If I surrender myself to Sheriff Bollinger, what is to prevent them from murdering me as well? It is true that, if I run, I may be running from the law until I die and I do not want that. Anne believes that I will be acquitted and says that she will marry me afterward and we will leave Hickman.

I do not know what to do. To give myself up to Bollinger would be like putting my head in a noose. There must be some other way.

The "other way" Clay chose was to surrender himself to the military post at Fort Nelson (two miles outside of Hickman) hoping, by this stratagem, to stay out of Brady's hands while, at the same time, remain on "the right side" of the law.

It soon became evident that he was not, in this way, to escape Brady's influence. The commander of the fort—a Captain Hooker—turned out to be one of Brady's "under-the-table" confreres who saw to it that Clay was imprisoned in a "bull pen" stockade, a small open area surrounded by high walls on which sentries were posted twenty-four hours a day. They "ironed" Clay—put shackles with chains on his ankles and wrists—and kept him staked to the ground all day every day, no matter what the weather. During this period, two toes on Clay's right foot became frostbitten, then gangrenous and had to be amputated by the post surgeon.

The trial was endlessly—deliberately, I feel—postponed in the hope that Clay would die of natural causes prior to the need for a trial. When his dogged will kept him alive, the trial was started.

Clay was forced to walk to the courthouse and back, the ankle irons rubbing at his skin until the flesh was lacerated, bleeding and infected. All hope deserted him as, first, McConnell, then Anne, left town without testifying on his behalf as promised. The trial was brief. Clay was found guilty of murdering the original Sheriff Bollinger and sentenced to hang.

Now in the custody of Bollinger's brother, he was mercilessly abused until he told a fellow prisoner that he anticipated hanging "with pleasure" so that his "torment would end."

One night in February, 1870, Bollinger, raging drunk, burst into Clay's cell and beat him almost senseless. He had just received notification from the office of the territorial governor that every man involved in the Brady-Courtwright War had been granted amnesty. Under the circumstances, Bollinger did not dare to murder Clay and, having beaten him savagely, threw him on a horse and sent him packing.

Barely conscious, slumped and bleeding on the saddle, Clay rode off into the darkness, heading toward the next phase of his life.

May 17, 1870

I have been in Caldwell now for two weeks. It is no great shakes of a town but it will do for a while. My money is holding out all right. I win a little at cards and lose a little. I can probably get by for several months without a job. I do not care to work right now. I am not in much condition to do so. I have not learned to walk very well yet with those two toes missing. Also, my ankles are weak and I get stiff in my back when the nights are cold. I am in great shape for a man of twenty-five years.

I am sitting in my room, writing in this book again. I decided to give it up after leaving Hickman. I did not care enough about day to day living to keep a journal on it. Now I feel a little better so I will start writing again.

I will not try to fill in the details of what happened to me after I gave myself up at Fort Nelson. (*The facts about this period were told to me by Clay, in person, at a later date. F.L.*) I will start here at Caldwell with a "new slate." Not that

I am a new *anything* myself. Leg wound, shoulder wound, missing toes, rheumatism, (I suppose that sounds like a poem!) from lying on that d——d ground so many days. It is amazing I can deal a hand of cards.

This town reminds me of Morgan City. It is similar in nature except for more permanent residents—about seven hundred. Morgan City only had four hundred. The look is the same, however, and the purpose. Caldwell is a cow town. I am told that more than a quarter of a million head of cattle move through its stockyards during shipping season.

The providing of entertainment for the men who drive the herds is Caldwell's main business. On South Main Street are four solid blocks of saloons, gambling and dance halls, fleabag hotels, cafes and w—— houses. The population of this "infamous zone" (as some old galoot I was drinking with called it) consists of w——s and horse thieves, drunks and murderers, cappers, deadbeats, and pickpockets, and close to a hundred gamblers, members of the so-called "circuit." It is a grand place to bring your mother for a visit.

If I could become good enough at cards to make a living, I would be pleased to join the "circuit" myself.

As the concluding sentence of this entry demonstrates, Clay, in his early days in Caldwell, despite a revival of his sense of humor, seemed to be retrograding toward that mental state which had given him trouble following the War and during his period of adventuring with Henry Blackstone.

Devoid of ambition, he passed his days without accomplishment, rising late and spending his afternoons and evenings playing cards and keeping company with the denizens of the four-block area along South Main Street.

This situation continued until one night when, while playing cards in an inebriated condition, he lost almost every cent he had and was forced to face the prospect of earning his keep once more.

While in this state, he took a conversation with some never-to-be-identified bartender and took a fateful step in the direc-

tion of the career which was, soon, to make his name a byword
in the West.

July 9, 1870

I have been thinking over seriously what that bar tender told
me last night.

He said that Caldwell has no law to speak of. Not that this
was much of a shock to me. It is clear the town is not con-
ducted on the order of a Sunday School. Still, I did not realize that the Marshal—a man named Palmer—has no control
at all, being merely a pawn in the hands of the local "merchants" who pay his salary, allow him to stay alive.

From what the bar tender said, Palmer is a coward and will
do anything to keep from following the former Marshals into
Boot Hill. (Four in all.)

The man in charge of everything is named Bob Keller. He
is the owner of the *Bullhead Saloon*—the biggest in the
town—and the president of The League of Proprietors—a
fancy way of saying "saloon owners."

I asked the bar tender if there are any Deputy Marshals and
he said that there are not. I am thinking of applying for the
job. If I can get in "on the deal" it will be fine with me. I am
sure there is enough money floating around to keep me from
starving. I am also sure that they could use a good man with
a gun to help them keep the peace during shipping season.

As is evident from this entry, Clay's motivation for desiring
to become a Deputy City Marshal in Caldwell was hardly of
the highest caliber, being more in the nature of a search for
an easy meal ticket than an ambition to foster law and order.
(At the same time, it is not surprising that Clay had no respect
for the principles of law and order in the West, having been
"stung" by them more than once.)

At any rate, learning a week later that the position of
Deputy Marshal was one which was handed out by the town

*council, he headed for the courthouse to consult the head of
said council, Mayor Oliver Weatherby Rayburn.*

July 11, 1870

I took a stroll to the courthouse after lunch today. It is a raw
pine structure on the edge of town.

There was a dried-up old man on the porch as I arrived. He
was sitting on a rocking chair, moving back and forth. He
looked a hundred years old. His derby hat was too big for his
shriveled head.

I asked him if he could tell me where to find Mayor Rayburn. The old geezer answered that he was "said dignitary."
(His own words.) I will try to remember the words he used
for he could sure spit out a power of them.

"May this ancient worthy inquire what he can do for you,
young man?" he asked.

I told him I had come to apply for the job of Deputy City
Marshal.

"If it is suicide you seek," he replied, "why not drink
or———— yourself to death for it is infinitely more pleasant to
pass on that way than with an aggravated case of lead poisoning."

It took me several moments to haul that in and sift out the
sense of it. Then I told him that I did not intend to commit
suicide but planned to rock on a porch myself some day, my
old head shaded by a derby hat. I said that I did not choose to
do manual work and was not good enough to be a professional gambler. (The fact that I was applying for a job was
proof enough of that!) As I had some skill with the gun and
did not buffalo easy (I told him) I figured I would not do too
badly as a Deputy Marshal. I assured him that I did not plan
to cause a wave of goodness and light to wash over Caldwell
but only wanted a "bread and butter" position.

He allowed as how he "apperceived my point of view" but
could not promise that Marshal Palmer would receive the
news of a new Deputy Marshal with smiles and songs. "Not

to mention Bob Keller and the League of Proprietors." He said that he liked me, however, and would appoint me if that was what I really wanted but that staying alive afterward was my problem.

I accepted and, I must say, for the first time since the attack on Mr. Courtwright's store, I felt a "tingle" of excitement. I hold that tingle precious after more than a year of deadness and would have gone on even if the job was not a paying one.

The mayor swore me in and told me to report to Marshal Palmer, who would more than likely be found at the *Bullhead Saloon* playing cards and drinking as a good, obedient peace officer should.

I went to the *Bullhead* and found the Marshal who is a red-necked, heavy man. I introduced myself and told him that I had just been appointed as his Deputy.

I can not say that my news went over big. Palmer looked at me as if I had just come crawling out of the nearest rat hole. The men who were playing cards with him seemed amused to hear it though, chuckling a good deal among themselves. One of these was Bob Keller, a big man with dark curly hair who, I guess, you would call handsome. All he had to say was that I limped kind of bad and did I think I could make my rounds without falling down?

I told him that I thought I could and Marshal Palmer got his voice back long enough to tell me I could take the night shift starting at six o'clock and lasting until midnight.

I played the whole hand like a farmer with hay seeds in his hair and I am sure they think I am some poor lad who has gone demented. From the way they started laughing when I left the saloon, I expect it was the joke of the year for them. This amuses me as I know what they do not—that they have got something on their hands a little more than expected. Not that I am going to turn on them and try to be a Big Man. But neither am I going to let them hurrah me. If they give me enough respect to get by on I will play along with them.

After I left the saloon, I took a walk around the South Main area, checking every entrance, front and rear, of every building. After that, I spent the last of my money on a shotgun and a saw which I took to my room. I have cut the barrel short and will take it with me on my "rounds."

I have also cleaned my revolver with extra care and spent about thirty minutes practicing my draw. I was pleased to see that I am not as creaky as I expected.

Now I am ready for my first time on the job as Deputy City Marshal of Caldwell, Texas. I do not think I will have too much trouble when they find out I am not planning to step on any toes.

Later: The job is not going to be as easy as I thought. I was prepared for a little trouble but not for what happened.

Promptly at six o'clock, I began to walk (limp) my rounds. I had pinned the badge on my shirt and, I must say, got many goggle-eyed stares from people I passed on South Main. I guess I am the first new "law man" they have seen in a month of Sundays.

All went well for about an hour. Then I heard the sound of gun shots coming from the *Bullhead Saloon* and, running over, saw what appeared to be a drunken cow boy staggering around inside, firing his revolver.

I say "what appeared to be a drunken cow boy" for, on the verge of going in, I got a prickling on the back of my neck and decided that I wasn't going to go in by the front way after all. I ran around the building as fast as I could and went in through the back.

My hunch proved correct. The drunk was only a ruse. Waiting in a front corner was a second man, gun drawn and cocked. The picture was clear to me. While I was trying to arrest the cow boy, the second man would give him back action and disarm me, maybe even kill me if I resisted.

Seeing this, I stepped in from the back room and held my revolver pointed at the second man, my shotgun at the first. "If you boys are itching to meet your Maker, now is the time to do it," I told them.

At that, the play was turned. That cow boy was no drunker than I was. He and the second man dropped their guns on the floor and raised their arms at my command. I glanced at Bob Keller who was sitting at a nearby table. (Palmer was "elsewhere.") I smiled and said, "Your boys will have to do better than that."

I do not know why I did not let it go at that. Bob Keller laughed and said that I had caught those men fair and square and there would be no more "horseplay" at my expense. He invited me to join him for a drink and I could tell, from his expression, that he expected me to do it.

I guess I am strange but I would rather have died than give him satisfaction at that point. He just *knew* that I was going to feel relieved and have that drink with him to be everlasting grateful for his kindness.

The look on his face when I told him that I couldn't have a drink with him until I had put the two men in jail was something to keep me warm on winter nights! His mouth fell open and he looked as if he had been kicked in the stomach by a mule.

He caught himself and smiled but I had won the hand and he knew it. He did not say any more as I marched those b——s to jail and locked them up.

That was not as easy to do as it is to write. It took me twenty-five minutes to find the key to the cell. That jail looks as though it hasn't had a cleaning in years, its only prisoners being spiders. I will have to clean it up, I can see. I had to laugh when the "drunken" cow boy sat on a cot and made a cloud of dust rise from the mattress that caused him to cough until his face was red.

Well, I have done it now. I could have "won over" Keller, I believe, but I had to do it my own way. Maybe I can settle things with him later. Right now I am sure he would be happy to see me take a one way ride to H———on a runaway horse.

All in all, a good day!

It is worth a comment, at this juncture, to point out Clay's intuitive ability to "smell" a perilous situation.

From a practical viewpoint, there can have been no logical reason for him not to enter Bob Keller's saloon when he saw what appeared to be a drunken cowboy firing indiscriminately.

Only if we look toward that sense which is "beyond the senses" can we explain Clay's action. This "extra" sense seems to have been part and parcel of the makeup of every successful gun fighter of that period. It is as if they had built in antennae which enabled them to "pick up" impulses of danger whether they were visible to them or not. This ability served Clay in good stead many times in the years to come.

As to his intention to "settle things" with Bob Keller, this was not to be, the entire situation altering radically the following day.

July 12, 1870

Things have sure moved fast since I had that talk with Mayor Rayburn yesterday!

I was in the jail this morning, sweeping up, when Palmer burst in, fortified by a breakfast of whiskey. Obviously, Keller had given him the word because he tried to order me to let the two men go and, when that didn't work, told me I was "discharged."

I know this kind. McConnell was exactly like him, all bluff and bluster and jelly for a spine. I told him he had better go back to Keller and tell him he had failed to follow orders properly. (It seems, no matter what my intentions, I end up "crossing swords" with Keller!)

Palmer started losing nerve and yelled at me in a voice that started sounding like a woman's. "You get out of here!" he cried. "No one wants you! Get out, d———it!"

I reached out and ripped the badge off his vest.

"No," I said. "*You* get out before I kick your——— to Kingdom Come."

He turned as white as a snowflake and left the office, moving backward. The next I heard, he had saddled up and ridden hell bent for leather out of town. I guess he knew his life was worthless from the moment he had failed to follow Keller's orders.

I finished cleaning the jail and took another walk to the courthouse. The good Mayor was still in his rocking chair. I think he has taken root there. I told him that since the position of City Marshal of Caldwell had been "vacated" unexpectedly, I was applying for the job.

He looked at the Marshal's badge which I had pinned to my shirt and nodded. "Since there seems to be no throng of applicants waiting to compete with you," he said, "I guess that your availability will decide the issue." (Lord, how that man can spiel!)

Then he leaned forward in his chair and said, "Young fellow, take it easy now and maybe you will see the Autumn."

I walked to the *Bullhead* and went inside. Keller was in his room so I went up and knocked on the door. He was with a woman and didn't like being disturbed. When I told him I was the new Marshal, that topped it. "The H———you are!" he said.

I guess I could have made some effort to unruffle his feathers. That was the time for it. There is something about him that rubs me the wrong way though. No matter what I mean to do, every time I see his face, I could not say a kind word if my life depended on it.

And it may.

The facts now stated were told to me by Clay at a later date, there being no way he could have known about them at the time.

After he had gone to Keller and informed him of his new status as City Marshal, Keller went storming to Mayor Rayburn who, not surprisingly, was also on his "boodle roll." He ordered Rayburn to get rid of Clay but Rayburn, old and tough—if not above whatever financial chicanery he could get away with—replied that Keller would have to do it himself.

There was no point in Keller arranging the "advent" of a new Mayor either, he added, because the new one might be even less cooperative than he.

He told Keller that it was better to leave well enough alone. Clay was far superior to Palmer and, during their peak season, a dependable Marshal would be valuable to "hold the cover on the boiling pot." As for Clay's antipathy toward Keller, that would pass and things would simmer down.

This proved to be an error in judgment on Mayor Rayburn's part. He did not take into consideration—perhaps the concept was beyond his limited intellectual means—the inimical chemistry between Clay and Keller.

Sometimes, two men cannot get along no matter what the circumstances. Why this is so is grist for a full-scale study in itself, being a matter of so many infinitesimal details and their admixture that no "pat" solution can possibly be advanced as to why such a clash occurs.

That it does occur is evident. Clay and Keller probably could not have made peace with each other if they tried. Some fundamental alienation existed between the two which, in time, resulted in one more step of the progression—or, some would say, retrogression—of Clay toward his ultimate station as one of the West's most noted men of violence.

Clay's initial days as City Marshal in Caldwell were not easy ones. His journal entries made it clear he felt compelled to prove that his authority was valid. With Keller doing everything in his power to thwart this effort, it turned out to be an onerous one indeed.

Clay began to experience, for the first time in his life, the uncomfortable sensation of knowing that his life was in jeopardy twenty-four hours a day. Shots burned by him in the night, fired from alleys or darkened windows. Near accidents occurred with horses, wagons, and falling objects. On at least one occasion he found ground glass in his food, on several others, scorpions in his bed, once, a rattlesnake.

This proved to be a far cry from the sort of excitement to which Clay responded. His "tingle" soon degenerated to a cold sweat, his pleasure at having achieved the position of City Marshal fading steadily. His nerves began to fray, his temper shortened.

Then, one day in September of that year . . .

September 7, 1870

Got a nice surprise today. While I was making my rounds, I ran into Cullen Baker and several of his cronies coming out of a saloon. He did not recognize me right away, seeming to see only the badge which made his features harden when I addressed him.

Then he remembered me and we shook hands. I invited him into the saloon for another drink but he said that he and his boys had to be on their way. I think his feeling toward me was unfriendly even though I tried to make him feel at home.

That is not important though. What is important is that, when I asked him where Henry was, he said in Kellville recovering from some minor buckshot wounds. Kellville is only forty miles away!

I have sent a letter with the evening stage and hope that Henry will receive it soon and answer me. I asked him if he would like to come to Caldwell and be my Deputy. I told him that I realized he had no love for the law (nor do I) but that being Deputy would be a good "cover" for him so that he could be safe from any warrant put out for his arrest. Also, I wrote that if he wanted action, this is the place to find it as a daily food.

G——, I hope he comes! It would be grand to see the "old fellow" again! It would also be a relief to have someone like him backing me up. I am getting tired of being alone. It is not good for the nerves.

The passage of several weeks of silence just about convinced Clay that either Henry had not received his message or did not choose to reply, feeling that Clay had betrayed their friendship by becoming a "law man." In this, he underestimated

Henry. To Blackstone, friendship was the only verity to be re-spected. He had no regard for anything else, least of all the law. It did not matter to him, therefore, which side of it he lived on. If "going honest" was what his friend requested, he would be pleased to do so.

September 23, 1870

Henry has come! G——— d——— but it is good to see his smiling face again! He has not changed a bit!

I was leaving my office when he came in.

"Well, old fellow," he said, "here I am."

I was so happy to see him I gave him a bear hug. He laughed and said to take it easy because his buckshot wounds were giving him a little bother.

I apologized and shook his hand. (*Wrung* his hand is what I did!) I had no idea how much I needed someone. When he told me he had come to be my Deputy, I felt a heavy weight fly off my back.

We talked a while and he told me what he had been doing since I last saw him. It was not much different from what he and I had done. How he can look so unchanged living like that is amazing to me.

He told me that he had read about my "exploits" in the Brady-Courtwright War which surprised me as I did not know that the papers in New Mexico had written about it. (How could I have known *anything* being staked to the ground every day?) He said that he had stopped in Hickman to say hello but found that I was gone. I told him all about it and he said that if he was ever back that way, he would shoot Bollinger for me.

I took him to the courthouse and told Rayburn I wanted Henry sworn in as my Deputy. Needless to say, the Mayor was rocking. He never even slowed down as he swore in Henry.

Henry and I walked back to South Main and went into the *Bullhead*. There, I introduced him to Keller. While that was still fresh in his craw, I told him he was going to have to move his faro tables out of the back room and put them in front where I could keep an eye on them. A lot of cow boys have complained to me that they were fleeced. His is not the only place that does it naturally but, since he is the biggest (and my favorite victim!), I figured an example should be set.

I really had the b——— off his balance today! To begin with, he is not sure at all how far he can push me. On top of that, Henry bothered the H——— out of him! I can see why. Henry looks so young—younger than me now—and standing there, smiling like he does, with a shotgun cradled in his arms, he must have set Keller's teeth on edge.

Maybe I imagined that but, whatever the case, they carried those tables into the front room and Henry and I left. We went across the street to the Palomino House and I bought him the biggest steak they had. Lord, but it is good to be together with him again!

Keller, now more anxious than ever to dispose of Clay— though unwilling to attempt the job himself—began to work on Lieutenant Alfred Gregory, the hot-tempered son of the General who commanded Fort Morgan, a nearby military post.

Gregory was well known in that area as a troublemaker. Handsome and arrogant, the victor in a score of past gun duels, he provided the ideal pawn for Keller's game.

Telling Gregory that Clay had voiced hostility toward him, he enhanced the plot by implying that the talk about Clay's prowess with the hand gun was without substance, no one ever really having seen him use it. As for the stories circulated by Henry Blackstone regarding the "murderous swath" Clay had cut through the Brady-Courtwright War in New Mexico, they were obvious fabrications put forth by Blackstone, with Clay's blessing, to bolster Clay's position as Marshal.

The first encounter between Gregory and Clay came about as follows.

November 19, 1870

I was standing at the counter in *The Virginia Saloon* tonight, having a drink with Henry when Lieutenant Gregory came in.

I knew as soon as I saw him that he had made up his mind to test me. Even as he started toward me, I made up *my* mind to try something I had never done before.

He stopped behind me and I turned to face him. Henry did not turn but watched us in the mirror. Knowing he was there gave me confidence that no tricks would be played on me.

"What do you want?" I asked Gregory.

"I want to know if you are really as fast with a gun as I have heard," he replied.

"There is only one way to find out," I said.

"That is why I am here," he answered. "I intend to prove to every one present that you are nothing but a bag of wind."

"Prove away," I told him.

"And after you are shot down, I am going to cut out your tongue and make you eat it before you die."

"Sounds as though you have quite an evening planned," I said. I did not look around but I knew Henry would be smiling at that.

Gregory waited.

"Well?" I asked. "What are you waiting for? If I am to have my tongue for a late snack, we had better get to it."

"Fill your hand," he said.

"I will not pull down on you first," I told him.

"You are a coward then," he said.

"No," I answered, "I am just too fast for you and think it only kind to let you take first crack."

That did it. I saw him start to draw in his eyes, long before the message reached his hand. I did not give him any time but snatched out my Colt and laid it across his skull as hard as I could. He went down like a sack of grain.

I finished my drink. Then Henry took one of Gregory's legs and I took the other and we dragged him out of the saloon and down the street to jail.

He opened his eyes as I was locking the door of the cell. I never saw such hatred in a man's face, not even Keller's. He told me that the next time we meet, the only possible exchange between us is one of lead.

I believe that I will not be able to buffalo him a second time and will keep my eyes on him in word and action.

Henry said that he did not know why I did not kill Gregory. I told him that I wanted to see if I could buffalo him as I had never done that to a man before. Henry asked me if I wanted him to kill Gregory in the cell but I told him no. I think he would have done it too.

Henry is as strange as ever.

The "show down" between Clay and Lieutenant Gregory came following a blizzard.

I wonder if the reader is aware of the fantastic violence of the so-called "Norther" of the plains. If not, it might not be amiss to append here a brief description of same selected from an article written by myself some years ago.

"The sky is a sunless gray and a deep, incredible stillness fills the air. Horses and cattle are restless, snorting and moaning in anticipation of something terrible about to happen.

"Suddenly, their breath goes white, all warmth swept from the air as a cloud of white appears on the horizon. Soft and fleecy-looking, it approaches quickly, rising and spreading. Soon the wail of wind is heard, the icy juggernaut drawing closer and closer.

"In the flash of an instant, it hits, a brutal "Norther"— blinding, smothering waves of fine white snow. Livestock turn their backs to it, covered, in seconds, by a blanket of white. Men, women and children rush for shelter, unable to breathe outside, their nostrils clogged by freezing, driving grains of snow, their eyes stung and blinded.

"The wind increases steadily, an Arctic banshee howling across the land. Nothing can be seen but one, continuous, glittering whirl of particles. Powdery snow rushes over everything. Great drifts begin to form. Horses and cattle shiver helplessly,

their mouths and eyelids frozen shut, icicles hanging from their jaws."

Such a blizzard hit Caldwell in December of that year leaving in its wake a vast, white, mantling silence.

Soon afterward, the incident which became popularly known as "Snowballs and Lead" occurred.

December 20, 1870

Henry and I were in the office, sitting by the stove, when we heard some horses stop outside. I was comfortable and sleepy so I asked Henry to see who it was.

He got up and went to the window.

"Gregory," he said.

That woke me quick enough. I got up and went over beside him.

Lieutenant Gregory and three men, one of them a Cavalry Sergeant, were just dismounting. They saw us looking at them but made no sign that they had. Their breath steamed as they stood outside, waiting.

"We have to go outside?" Henry asked.

"Don't you want to?" I said.

"No," he replied. "It is too cold. Can't we just shoot them down from here?"

"Henry," I said. "We are law men. We are supposed to *not* shoot people if we can."

"I thought you said this job was going to be fun," he replied. I glanced at him. Naturally, he was smiling.

We looked at Gregory and the three men for a while. I guess they thought we were trying to figure out a way to get out of it.

"If we can keep from going out a little longer," I said, "they will freeze to death and we will not have to face them."

"I hope so," Henry said. "I hate to go outside when it's cold."

"Well," I said after a few more moments, "we had better go out anyway."

We put on our coats and hats but no gloves.

"The odds are not good," I said. "If we can keep from shooting, we had better do it."

"Anything you say," Henry told me but I knew that he was hoping there would be gun play. There is a difference in his smile when he is ready for action. I did not notice it in the old days but I do now.

We went outside and stood on the plank walk facing the four men across the hitching pole. There was snow on top of it and I scooped up some and started packing a snow ball while we talked.

"Well," I said, "don't you think it is a little cold for this sort of thing?"

"Don't worry," Gregory said, "you will be frying in H——— pretty quick."

"Has it ever occurred to you that *you* might be the one to fry?" I asked.

"No," he said. "It is going to be you and your G——— d———d, grinning Deputy."

I looked at the other men. They did not seem as sure of the play so I decided to work on them. If I could separate them from Gregory, there would be less of a problem.

"You boys look sensible," I said. "Why are you here? This is not your ruckus."

None of them spoke but I could see, clear enough, that not one of them wanted to fight.

"We are not here to listen to you, you yellow b———," Gregory said. I saw him pull back the flap of his coat and start to draw and I let fly with the snow ball. It was a risk but it worked. The snow ball hit him on the hand and knocked his revolver into the snow.

The Sergeant knew what I was trying to do right away. It is strange how he and I seemed to understand each other without a word between us while, after seven months of talk, Keller and I are further apart than ever.

Any way, the Sergeant understood that I was trying to avoid spilling blood and, as quick as he could, he snatched up snow, rolled a ball and heaved it at me. It hit me on the chest and splattered over my coat.

That opened up the situation fine. Those other men were glad to grab up snow and, in a matter of seconds, the air was thick with snow balls flying back and forth. Everybody started laughing. Henry got a real kick out of it and laughed louder than any of them. We started having a H——— of a good time and I figured I had saved some lives.

Henry broke it. I do not know if it was an accident or not. I am afraid it wasn't because Gregory had called him a G——— d——d, grinning Deputy. Henry kept throwing snow balls at him. Gregory was not returning them but he was not shooting either even though he had picked up his gun and put it back in its scabbard. He was smart enough to know that it wasn't four to two in his favor anymore but two to one in ours.

As I say, Henry broke it. First, he knocked off Gregory's hat. That was not too bad as I had lost my hat as well as the Sergeant and one of Gregory's other men. But then Henry hit Gregory full in the face with a snow ball and blood started spurting from Gregory's nose as he staggered back. It must have hurt him something terrible.

"You G——— d——d s——— of a b———!" he cried. Suddenly, he did not seem to care what the odds were for he snatched at his revolver.

I guess that was what Henry was waiting for. He outdrew Gregory and shot him dead between the eyes.

In that moment, all the fun and laughter ended. The three men went for their revolvers, I drew mine and gun fire exploded all around. It did not last for more than five or six seconds, I believe. When the cloud of black smoke drifted off, Henry and I were still on our feet, untouched, but, except for us, only the Sergeant was still alive and that was because I had tried to knock him down without killing him.

I put my Colt away and moved to the Sergeant. The snow was red with his blood.

"I am sorry it went this way," I said. "You saw I was trying to avoid it."

He nodded but could not speak because of pain. I helped him to his feet and started leading him down the street toward Doctor Kiley's place. Henry went with me.

As we passed the *Bullhead*, Keller and some other men were standing outside. Keller glared at us, disappointed that we were still alive.

"The next time you talk anybody into coming after me," I told him, "I will come gunning for you after I have killed them."

He did not say any thing. He jumped as Henry kicked some snow across his legs and shoes. He would not fight though. Henry kicked some more snow at him and he backed away. When Henry picked up snow, Keller went into his saloon fast. Henry threw a snow ball after him which sailed over the bat wing doors. I hope it hit him on the back of the head but I doubt it.

The next time I *will* go after him, the miserable s———of a b———. The Sergeant died tonight. It is a waste of a good man. I promised him that I would write to his wife in St. Louis. I wish I knew what I could say to her that would make it easier.

The duel in the snow was the first gunbattle of Clay's to be publicized to any extent.

While some notoriety had attached itself to his part in the Brady-Courtwright War, word of it was not as widely promulgated as word of this particular encounter.

Why this is so is anybody's guess. My personal feeling is that the details of it had a certain extra color to them: a good-looking young Marshal trying to avoid bloodshed by at tempting to convert a moment of sanguine threat into one of schoolboy jollity and, failing that, making it obvious that the attempt had not been motivated by cowardice by revealing himself to be a deadly gun handler and, with his Deputy, killing three men and fatally wounding a fourth, all at close range.

Whatever the reason, the story of "Snowballs and Lead" spread around the country like wildfire, catching the fancy of a man who, more than anyone, was to catapult Clay's name into national prominence.

April 17, 1871

Henry and I were having breakfast at the Palomino House when this dude came in and walked over to our table.

He introduced himself as Miles Radaker, the editor-publisher of a New York City magazine called *The Current Observer.*

I asked him what he was doing so far away from his home digs.

He told me that he had come out West for a number of reasons. The main one was to meet me.

"What for?" I asked.

"You are too modest, sir," he replied. "Do you not realize that your name is on everyone's tongue back East?"

"Why?" I asked.

"Because of your heroic exploit in the snow," he said. "Not to mention your daring accomplishments during the Brady-Courtwright War on which I have been doing considerable research."

"Is that right?" I said.

"That is pre-eminently right, sir," he replied. (He and Mayor Rayburn ought to get together!) "People back East are entranced by frontier activities and read every word about them they can lay their hands on. And you, sir, are just the sort of man they want to read about."

He sounded weird to me so I did not have too much to say to him. I left, soon, to go to the office. Henry stayed behind. I wish I could have hidden underneath the table and listened. Henry said, later, that he started telling Radaker one "whopper" after another about me. For once in his life, he said, he did not smile but kept a serious face.

For instance, Radaker asked him how many men I had killed.

"Well, sir," Henry answered, "not counting Rebs and Indians, seventy-five. No, make that seventy-six. I forgot the one he shot this morning before breakfast. He likes to do that as it sharpens his appetite."

How he could keep a straight face through that I can not imagine. When he told me all the crazy things he had said, to Radaker, about me, I laughed until my sides ached.

What is most amazing, Henry said, is that Radaker believed every word!

Here, Henry Blackstone (and Clay) revealed his basic naivete.

I know Miles Radaker and, if there is one quality he does not possess to any degree whatsoever it is gullibility. Obviously, Blackstone, thinking he was joshing Radaker, was, in fact, being joshed himself. I have no doubt that Radaker knew that Blackstone was "stretching the truth," but did not care since this was exactly the sort of material he was looking for. The more outrageous the lies, he knew, the more they would work to his advantage. To Blackstone, he may have appeared gratifyingly agog. Actually, I am sure that Radaker was mentally adding up the dollars to come even as he listened, openmouthed and "credulous," to Blackstone.

All unknowingly, therefore, thinking that he was only joking, Henry Blackstone began to build that structure of fictional absurdities upon which Clay was soon to climb to fame's precarious heights.

Let me be clear on this. Clay was as I have presented him; to all intents and purposes, fearless in a dangerous situation and, without a doubt, deadly with a six-shooter. He was not the Godlike figure all the stories make him out to be. No human being ever could be such a figure and Clay was human; very human.

The first articles in Radaker's magazine appeared that summer.

July 9, 1871

That dude, Radaker, was not joking when he said that he was going to write an article about me in his magazine.

Today, the stage brought in a copy of the magazine with

the article in it. Radaker sent it to me. It is a caution sure enough.

Henry read it to me in the office this evening. I had already looked it over but the true foolishness of it was not apparent until Henry read it aloud.

"This Halser," he read, "has one of the handsomest physiques that I have ever had the pleasure to observe. His shoulders are incredibly broad and taper to a narrow waist at which hangs his brace of 'forty-fives,' ever ready for action."

I was trying to get some paperwork done and I told Henry to shut up. *Brace of forty-fives!* Radaker must have been blind not to see that I only wear one gun and it is a .41.

Henry would not shut up. "There is grace and dignity in his manly carriage," he read on. "His face is exceptionally well-fashioned by the Creator's art, his lips thin and artistically sensitive, his nose a strong, aquiline promontory, his eyes as gentle as . . ."

Henry snorted and almost fell off his chair, which was leaning against the wall. ". . . as a woman's!" he said.

I had to laugh. *"Will you shut up?"* I said.

He would not. There were tears rolling down his cheeks as he kept on reading. "One would not believe that these two gentle orbs have pointed the way to dusty death for scores of frontier miscreants. [That word really tied his tongue in a knot.] But, as they say on the border: When Halser shoots, it is to kill."

"Shut up!" I yelled and threw my hat at him. He fell off his chair and landed on the floor, kicking his legs he was laughing so hard.

I have thought about it all day and, I must say, it is not only amusement I feel. I suppose I can not blame Henry for telling those whoppers to Radaker. He meant no harm and, even if he had not told them, Radaker probably would have written the article any way.

Still, I am displeased. The article makes me sound foolish. I may not be a Great Hero but I am not a fool. And I *have* done *some* of the things he wrote of in the article. It is just that they are lost in all those lies.

* * *

Two facts become apparent from this entry:

One: Clay resented the exaggerations, being honest enough to recognize them for what they were.

Two: This resentment was equally directed at the fact that the article tended to obscure those of his achievements which were true.

In brief, he did not mind being placed in the limelight but wanted facts to put him there, not fancies.

I speak from firsthand knowledge when I state that Clay was not immune to the gratification of being celebrated. In the early days of his newborn renown, he was not at all adverse to being famous, only to being famous for the wrong reasons.

The possibility that this spurious acclaim might be a source of danger did not occur to him.

About that time, an old acquaintance returned to his life.

July 25, 1871

Got a nice surprise today. The Fenway Circus has come to Caldwell.

I was in the office when the wagons rolled by. I did not see Hazel but I saw the name of the circus.

After having dinner, I took a stroll to the edge of town where they were setting up the tent. Seeing my badge, Fenway thought I was there to make problems but I told him that he was welcome in Caldwell and asked him if Hazel and Carl were still with his show.

He said that they were but that Carl was now a ground worker and Hazel has another partner for the act.

He told me where to find her wagon and I went there. Carl was working, helping to set up the tent. I walked right by him but he did not recognize me. He looks terrible. He must be drinking more than ever.

I knocked on the door of the wagon and Hazel asked who it was.

"Clay Halser," I said.

She was silent long enough to tell me that she didn't remember my name. Then she said, "Clay!" and pulled open the door. She had been drinking some herself. Maybe that was why she didn't recall me.

I went inside and we kissed each other. She had only a thin robe on and the way she pressed against me I could feel every soft part of her.

She said that Carl would be working for hours and she bolted the door and took off her robe less than a minute after I got in the wagon.

I was worried about Carl but she said not to be as she took my clothes off. She said that even if he came in while we were "at it" he would not say a word. She takes care of him now, providing him with whiskey and a place to sleep. (Never her bed anymore.)

I had forgotten how good it was with her. Nancy and Myra at Mama Wilkie's place are not bad but nothing special. Hazel is special. I hope the circus stays here for a long time.

She is impressed that I am the City Marshal in Caldwell. She hinted that she is getting tired of circus life and of Carl and that a man "in my position" could use a "help mate."

I suppose that is true but I do not think that Hazel is the one. She is still married to Carl for one thing and, even if she was not, I do not think that I would care to make her Mrs. Halser. She is starting to look a little "worn at the seams" as they say and she is so willing to get into bed with me that I suspect she has gotten into bed with many other men too.

I wonder if it would make any sense to write to Mary Jane. I guess not. I am sure she is married already.

I would write to Anne if she had not betrayed me. I still have a warm place in my heart for her despite her treachery. Maybe treachery is too hard a word for what she did. What difference does it make? I will never see her again.

Any way, Hazel will save me the money I usually spend at Mama Wilkie's!

* * *

*At this point, I can break in personally, not only to com-
ment on Clay's journal but to carry forward the story for a
period of time.*

*In the summer of that year, I traveled to Caldwell to inter-
view Clay. Having read Radaker's outlandish article, I recognized the unbelievable figure presented as being none other
than the present day (exaggerated) version of the young sol-
dier I had interviewed near the end of the War.*

I persuaded my editor (I worked, at that time, for The Greenvale Review) *to let me travel West, speak to Clay and prepare
a series of articles which, while no less fascinating, would be
more factual and, therefore, more acceptable to the intelligent
reader. Fortunately, I was able to convince him—because
of personal experience—that Radaker's article was not completely false, only colored to a ludicrous extent. I assured my
editor that a more realistic approach would prove even more
popular; that, within the boundaries of truth, Clay had accomplished many things well worth recording.*

*I was witness to such an occurrence one afternoon while
talking to Clay in a saloon. A cowboy (later identified as the
one who had pretended to be drunk on Clay's first night as
Deputy Marshal) walked up behind Clay, drew out his revolver
and pressed it to the back of Clay's head.*

*"Now I got you, Mr. Marshal Big Time Halser," he said.
"Let me see you get out of this tight."*

*While I observed in speechless dread, Clay replied, "Now,
Jim, that is not your way. You are not the kind to take a man's
life without giving him a show."*

*I do not know which aspect of the situation shocked me
more—the sight of that cowboy with the muzzle of his revolver
pressed against the back of Clay's head or Clay's incredibly
calm voice. He might have been ordering dessert in a restaurant!*

*"We have no reason to be set against each other, Jim," he
said. "We both know it is Keller who wants me dead because
I am trying to prevent him from cheating men like you in
crooked card games. You and I have every reason to be*

friends so why not put up your gun and sit down to split a bottle of champagne with me?"

I cannot put down every word Clay said because, in truth, I cannot remember them. The words above I wrote from memory that very evening. Even at that, I could not remember every word because there were too many of them—although the foregoing conveys the "gist" of their import. Clay kept telling the cowboy, over and over, that he was a person of honor who would not murder a defenseless man; that Keller was the one behind the situation and that there was no reason for the cowboy and Clay not to be the best of friends; finally, that Clay would be honored if the man would sit down with him and split a bottle of champagne. In the deathly silence of that saloon, Clay must have spoken without cease for a good twenty minutes before the cowboy pulled back his revolver and put it away.

At that, Clay moved for the first time, turning casually to the bartender and ordering a bottle of champagne. This was brought to the table where Clay poured some for me, the cowboy and himself. What is more, I swear on the Bible that there was not so much as a tremor to his hand!

He toasted the cowboy ("You are the right stripe of man, Jim."), had a few glasses of champagne, exchanged several jokes, then left.

I followed him to his hotel room.

"Who is it?" he asked when I knocked on the door.

I told him and he unlocked the door to let me in.

He had just taken off his coat and vest and was in the process of removing his shirt. He might have just come in from standing in a rainstorm, it was so sopping wet.

"That was inspiring," I told him.

Clay smiled. "Perspiring," he said.

Notwithstanding, I was genuinely impressed and made haste to convey that feeling in the first of my projected series of articles for the The Greenvale Review.

When it appeared in the magazine a few months later, I was appalled by the changes made. It had been enlarged upon and, like the Radaker article, conveyed a general tone of grandiloquent hero worship. What I had intended to be an honest appraisal turned out to be merely another slice of lurid journalism.

Infuriated, I resigned my position with the magazine and vowed never to attempt such an article again. (Unfortunately, by then, I had already sent in two more which were, also, "doctored" beyond recognition.) I apologized to Clay, who accepted with grace. Again, however, I could see that, while amused by the article's excesses, he could not help but be affected by the fact that all those sumptuous words were about him.

I remained in Caldwell for a number of months, working for the local paper, (The Caldwell Gazette) *a position which Clay acquired for me.*

It was not my intention to remain in Caldwell indefinitely but to stay there only long enough to collect an adequate amount of material regarding Clay, so that I might prepare a biography of his life. In this way, I hoped to be able to present, to the reading world, a more honest examination of his achievements.

It is to my shame that, to this day, no such biography has been written. (One reason, perhaps, I have prepared this volume.) Nonetheless, the period during which I lived in Caldwell did enable me to observe, at first hand, the rise of the Halser Legend.

After Radaker's article—and mine, I presume—had "started the wheels turning," an increasing number of magazines and newspapers sent representatives to Caldwell to interview Clay. He had "caught on" in the East as a symbol of Heroism. He was Hercules in boots, Samson with "a brace of pistols." (I never did know whether Clay's eventual practice of wearing two six-shooters was a matter of practicality or an unconscious desire to match the descriptions of himself which invariably referred to "a forty-five in each hand, spewing leaden death to all who opposed him.")

At any rate, Clay was plucked from the crowd by the hand of a thrill-loving populace and lifted to a height of dubious fame. Men everywhere began to envy him, women to dream romantically of him. He became an idol to the young.

Much to my uneasiness, I saw that he was starting to acquire a kind of helpless fascination toward the mounting flood of written matter concerning him. It was as if he read the articles and stories with a schism in his mind. For a time, he would be amused by the absurdities of what was written. Then, it seemed, it would rush across him that he was reading about himself; that all those words of praise and reverence were about him and no other—and he would react accordingly.

When the novels started to appear, his absorption became indelible. How many men, in their middle twenties, have novels written about them?—full-length books which refer to them by name, in which they are involved in one incredibly heroic exploit after another? Even discerning their flaws with a clear eye—which he never lost—he could not restrain an inward sense of pleasure. (Indeed, had he been able to do so, he really would *have been a Super Being.)*

Soon, a reaction began to manifest itself and he found himself becoming edgy and defensive. In essence, his rationale (though never actually voiced) might have been: "All right, the articles, and stories, and books are ridiculous exaggerations. Still they are not entirely made up. I have not exactly been sitting on my hands since leaving Pine Grove. Some of what they are writing is true.

"Quite a bit of it, in fact."

I have, deliberately, omitted, from this section of the story, the many journal entries which detail the day-by-day problems Clay faced as Marshal of Caldwell. I have done this primarily because they, largely, duplicate a later section of this book in which the elements of being Marshal in a "cow town" are more, graphically, covered.

Suffice to say that Clay's conflict with Keller continued unabated. Keller was never resigned to Clay's position as Marshal. Clay trod upon his toes on too many occasions, costing him money.

In addition to this conflict, there was, of course, the main body of Clay's duties which was to "keep the peace" (as well as he could) when the masses of cowboys descended on the town like locusts following their drives to the rail head. These periods were incredibly demanding. During them, he and Henry Blackstone were forced to be "on call" virtually twenty-four hours a day. Clay made some attempt to ease this situation; by swearing in additional deputies during these times but, almost always, they would quit when the "going" became too hard for them.

About this time, reactions to the laudatory articles about Clay began to occur periodically when cowboys, their courage fired by whiskey, would challenge Clay to gun fights.

On almost every one of these occassions, Clay used, to great advantage, his ability to "buffalo" his would-be opponents. Outdrawing them, he would knock them unconscious with the barrel of his revolver, toss them into jail, and release them the following morning, chastened and, almost always, grateful for his forbearance in not killing them.

On one occasion, however, when a cowboy tried, again, to "take him on" the next day, Clay was forced to shoot him. Fortunately, the cowboy's wound was not severe and, after a period of recuperation, he was able to return to the ranch on which he worked.

Clay ultimately solved the problem almost altogether by initiating a "no guns while in town" policy which, following some inevitable resistance, was generally accepted.

Finally, I have eliminated those entries which mention Clay's renewed dalliance with Hazel Thatcher.

During the time the circus was in Caldwell, he and she "took up" where they had left off in Morgan City. Their relationship was marked by a total lack of growth. Although Hazel suggested, more than once, the advantages she foresaw in a marriage between them, Clay never went along with her. Clearly, his moral standards would not permit him to associate with such a woman in marriage although he was perfectly willing to share her company and bed as long as she permitted it.

I might add that I am not able to appreciate how she could have been described, by Clay, as a "powerfully good-looking woman." Even allowing for the deterioration which attends "hard" living, I do not see how a truly "good-looking" woman could have lost so much in her appearance (between that time and the time they first had met in Morgan City), as to look the way Hazel Thatcher did when I knew her. "Coarse" is the only word which comes to mind.

In time, the circus left and there was a rather cool farewell between the two.

Soon after—as an unexpected dividend of his mounting fame—a relationship more meaningful in Clay's life was restored.

March 14, 1872

I am very excited and happy as I write this. I received a letter from Anne today!

I always hoped that I would hear from her again although I never really could believe that I would.

Now I have and I understand why she did not testify at my trial.

She explained that, after her father had run out (in the dead of night while she and her stepmother were asleep!) her stepmother had run off with another man and ended up, sick and destitute, hundreds of miles away. She had written to Anne for help and Anne had traveled to her side to remain with her for several months, nursing her back to health.

She had had every intention of testifying for me but her correspondent from Hickman—a Brady sympathizer she eventually discovered—had lied to her about the trial date. When she'd finally learned of my conviction, she had made immediate plans to return to Hickman despite her stepmother's illness.

Then she had been told about the Governor's amnesty and had assumed that I was safe and would wait for her despite the fact that I had failed to answer any of her letters. (I never received one of them and am convinced that they were destroyed before I could.)

Now she has read about me in the newspaper and "taken courage in hand" to write to me. She hopes that I remember her kindly and will come to visit her in Hickman some day.

I still love you very much is the final sentence of her letter.

My G————, I am happy! I have sent her a letter, telling her that I still love her too and want her to marry me and come back to Caldwell with me as my wife.

Things are slow now any way. I can make Henry temporary marshal while I travel to Hickman.

Anne!

Clay received a prompt, overjoyed answer from Anne and immediately prepared to entrain to Hickman.

Since I was planning to return to New York about that time, I arranged my schedule so that he and I could ride North together before going our separate ways.

A minor—yet telling—incident occurred our second day out.

Two young boys, discovering that Clay was on the train, approached him, saucer-eyed, to stare and listen reverently to his words.

Embarrassed by their gaping awe—especially with me sitting beside him and the other passengers observing—Clay resorted to the tall tale, spinning the boys a whopper in which fifty-seven Indians trapped him in a box canyon with his only weapon a knife.

"What happened?" *asked one of the boys.*

"I was killed," *Clay answered.*

His intent had, clearly, been to josh the boys out of their attitude of hero worship and give them a laugh. Instead, all he did was confuse them. I am sure that they believed that Clay had been telling them the gospel truth until his final words, at which point, for some unexplainable reason, he had chosen to avoid relating the gory details of how he had killed those fifty-seven savages with his knife.

As they returned to their mother, disappointed, Clay

frowned and said he did not understand. It was the one time in all the years I knew him that I directed a remark at him which might have been interpreted as critical.

"You almost believe some of the stories yourself now," I said. "Is it any wonder that they believe them all?"

Clay and Anne were reunited to discover that the fervor of their love was easily recaptured.

Clay remained in Hickman for a month, at the end of which time he and Anne were married in the community church and prepared to return to Caldwell.

Another telling incident occurred the day they went to leave Hickman.

May 2, 1872

I cleaned out an old sore today.

Anne and I were on our way to the train station when I caught sight of Sheriff Bollinger talking to some men across the street.

I stopped the carriage and told Anne that I would be right back. I crossed the street and walked up to Bollinger.

"There you are, you son of a b———," I said. "I have been wondering where you have been hiding while I was in town."

The man is a coward. I have always known that. All the blood in his face disappeared. He stared at me with the look of a man who knows he is about to die.

I did not try to change that look.

"You yellow b———," I said. "Maybe you would like to beat me now."

He raised his arms as though I had said, "Hands up." "I have no quarrel with you," he said.

"Well, I have a quarrel with you," I said. "And I am going to end it here and now. Go for your gun, you son of a b———."

"No," he said. "I have no quarrel with you."

"Either go for your gun or I will shoot you down like the dog you are," I told him.

"You would not shoot a man with his hands in the air, would you?" he asked.

"What makes you think you are a man?" I said. "You are a sneaking cur and a bully, nothing more."

Sweat was running down his face. He looked sick to his stomach.

"Are you going to fill your hand?" I asked. "Or must I murder you?"

"You would not," he said. "You would not."

I was getting tired of it by then. What glory is there in humbling such a specimen?

"Tell these men here that you are a coward and a G—— —— d————d son of a b————," I told him.

He said it right away as if he believed it.

"Now take off your gun belt and drop it in that water trough," I said.

He unbuckled his belt with shaking hands and dropped the works into the water.

"If I ever hear of you wearing a gun again," I said, "I will come back and kill you without mercy."

I turned on my heel and went back to Anne. I think that Bollinger will not be very popular in Hickman now.

While Clay, perhaps, deserved some praise for his restraint in not actually killing Bollinger, he failed to realize, I believe, that, to a large degree (if not entirely), Bollinger was cowed so pitifully by Halser the Legend rather than by Halser the man.

It is, of course, possible that Bollinger, being what he was, might have behaved in just as craven a manner had there not been any articles or stories recounting Clay's deadly skill with a gun.

I very much suspect, however, that the stories had *affected Bollinger and that he believed himself to be confronted by some Super Being at whose dread hand he could expect no mercy.*

May 9, 1872

This has been the roughest day I have spent in Caldwell since the day Lieutenant Gregory rode into town to kill me.

I have told Anne that it can not happen again but I do not think she believes me. It is too bad it had to take place the first day she arrived here.

Henry did not write to me while I was in Hickman but that did not disturb me. I assumed that he had things in hand.

I had a bad surprise in store when we reached the hotel. Anne and I had been stared at while we were walking from the train station but I figured that it was because they had heard I was getting married and were curious about my wife.

It turned out to be a different story altogether.

Claxton (*the desk clerk. F.L.*) was amazed to see me! He said that every one thought I had left Caldwell for good. I asked him how they could think that. Did they believe that I had made Henry the Marshal?

That brought on the second bad surprise. Henry left town two weeks ago, he told us! (To this moment, I do not know why.) The third bad surprise—a new Marshal had been sworn in by the Mayor!

I got Anne set up in a room and told her I would be back as soon as I had settled things. She seemed upset and I could not blame her. She must have thought that I had made up the whole thing about being Marshal of Caldwell!! Now that I look back, she must have thought, for a while, that she had married a mad man!

I walked to the courthouse. For a change, Rayburn was not on the porch, sitting on his beloved rocking chair. I found him inside, in his office and asked him what the H———— was going on.

He looked surprised to see me too. He said that, like every one else, he had thought that I had left Caldwell for good—especially after Henry took out.

I asked him who had told him all this. I should have known.

Bob Keller.

Rayburn told me that the new Marshal was one of Keller's "toadies" just as Palmer had been.

"We will see about that," I said.

"I don't think that Keller is going to be glad to see you," Rayburn told me.

"I do not give a d——— whether he is glad or not," I said. "I am the Marshal and that is the way it is going to remain."

I was seeing red by then. I walked fast as I could to the *Bullhead* knowing that, whoever the new "Marshal" was, he would be there.

He was at that. I found him playing cards with a few of Keller's other boys. If I had not been so mad, I would have laughed. It was Nicholson! *(The other man Clay had put in jail his first night as Deputy Marshal. F.L.)*

He looked pretty d——d surprised to see me. I walked across the room to the table he was sitting at. He was about to take a drink of whiskey and the glass was frozen in the air between the table and his mouth. I knocked it out of his hand and grabbed him by the shirt front. Hauling him to his feet, I ripped the badge off his shirt and shoved him back into the chair.

"If you want it back," I told him, "you will have to take it from my dead fingers."

I waited for him to draw but was not surprised when he did not. He started to shake and put his hands on the table, palms down.

"Who in the H ——— told you that you could be the Marshal?" I demanded.

"Mr. Keller," he replied. "He told me that you were gone for good. I swear I would not have put on the badge if I had known you were coming back."

I had to believe him because he was so scared.

Just then, Keller came down from upstairs and I walked over to him.

"If you ever try to pull a trick like that on me again," I told him, "I will bury you in Boot Hill."

He did not answer me but I could see, in his eyes, that he was close to the edge.

To make sure he could not back down, I told him that, from then on, I was going to hurrah him night and day. "I am going to make a set of rules for you alone," I said. "And if you break just one of them, I will toss you in the hoosegow and throw away the key."

I turned and started for the door, using the sides of my eyes to keep a watch on him in the wall mirror.

As I expected, I was almost to the door when he reached beneath his coat to draw the Derringer I knew was there.

Before he could fire, I dove to the left and took shelter behind the counter end as the shot roared and a ball tore wood away near my head.

Snatching out my gun, I reached above the counter and fired back at him. I heard chairs scraping back and men running for safety.

"Nicholson!" Keller shouted.

I thought he was asking Nicholson to assist him in killing me and I shouted, "Any man who helps Keller is a dead one!"

Another shot rang out and lead exploded through the wood close to me. I flung myself behind the counter and the bar tender took off. I did not realize, at that moment, that Keller had called to Nicholson to throw him his six-shooter.

Another shot roared and bottles were smashed above me, spilling whiskey on me. I looked up and saw a movement in the mirror. Keller was rushing toward the end of the counter to shoot at me.

I reared up fast. He was just passing by. I saw his head snap around, a look of shock on his face. Then I fired at point blank range and put two balls in his heart. He was flung away from the counter and landed, dead, on the floor, his vest on fire.

I looked around the room but all the others had gone. Keeping my Colt in hand just to be safe, I edged along the wall. I saw the bar tender peering out from the back room and told him to "put out" his boss.

I returned to the hotel. My clothes were dirty and wrinkled and there was a tear in the right knee of my trousers. Anne, who had heard the gun fire, was waiting on the porch of the hotel, looking terrified. I took her by the arm and led her back inside.

"Is this the way it *always* is?" she asked.

I had to chuckle at the sound of her voice. She sounded like a little girl.

"It will simmer down now," I told her.

Simmer down it did. Keller disposed of, all organized attempts to weaken Clay's position ceased and, within the framework of what it was—a "wild and woolly" frontier cattle town—Caldwell assumed almost a tranquil atmosphere. Clay had succeeded in "taming" it.

He had, also, succeeded in creating, for himself, a state of gilt-edged boredom. Violence and tension, he discovered, are like drugs to which a man of his temperament can become addicted.

The articles and stories and books continued, but the situations which inspired them no longer occurred—or occurred in such minor ways as to be without stimulation to him. As in Pine Grove, seven years earlier, he started to become restless and discontented, yearning for renewed excitement to "get his blood moving" again. (Clay's own phrase.)

This situation was exaggerated by the problems inherent in the establishment of a marriage relationship with Anne. Always in the past, Clay had sought out the company of women only when he needed to assert his "male prerogative." He had never been required to make allowances for female tastes or desires. Now, he did, and it is probable that these emotional demands on him caused him to yearn, all the more, for some escape from marital responsibilities. It is even possible that what he sought was an escape from marriage itself, using his desire for action as an excuse to separate himself from the obligations of matrimony. With Henry gone (and unheard from) he did not even have a "crony" to share his troubles with. Card games were out. Drinking was out. Fighting was out. Accordingly, to Clay's way of thinking, enjoyment of life was out.

When a letter arrived, from the City Council of Hays,

Kansas, offering him the job of peace officer, he was immediately eager to accept. The deterrent was Anne. Despite the fact that the offer was, financially, a better one, she was opposed to accepting it. With a baby on the way, she wanted to live in a settled community. Caldwell might not be "exciting" anymore but it was maturing sensibly. As a charter citizen, Clay should be investing in its future, planning toward a quiet, affluent retirement.

It is my personal observation that Anne Halser never understood her husband's needs. A "typical" young woman, she desired a home, a family, and security. While, certainly, no criticism can be leveled at her for aspiring to these age-old desires, at the same time I believe that she should have realized that a marriage to Clay could not possibly bestow these things on her.

Her desire to remain in Caldwell and "live a quiet life" was, undoubtedly, more chilling a prospect to Clay than the prospect of facing those "fifty-seven Indians" with a knife would have been. His entries, during this period, consist, almost entirely, of reasons why the offered job was superior to his present one and why Anne should be able to "see" it.

Where his position in Caldwell brought in a salary of one hundred and twenty-five dollars per month, the new one guaranteed one hundred and fifty. Where the portion of fines he received in Caldwell was ten per cent, in Hays he would receive twenty-five. Where they had to live in the hotel in Caldwell (they could have moved into a house eventually, of course; Clay was "loading" the situation there), in Hays they would be given a house. If Anne was really concerned about the needs of their coming children, she should appreciate the value of the new job.

Anne's reply (unfortunately, for Clay, a devastatingly valid one) was that their main consideration should be the need of their children to see their father remain alive and not shot down in the street.

It took ten months for Clay to win the argument. After their baby—a girl which they named Melanie—was born and Anne could no longer use the argument that she did not want to travel while carrying the child, Clay renewed his attack, now almost threateningly, his boredom in Caldwell having reached a fever pitch by then.

Finally, Anne succumbed although convinced that Clay was making a terrible mistake. An entry made at this time is revealing.

March 14, 1873

Anne is in bed, upset. We have had another argument.

She said something that disturbs me. I can not believe it to be true and yet it bothers me.

I told her that I feel it is my responsibility to bring law and order to Hays as there are not many men who can.

"It isn't law and order you care about!" she cried. "You are just searching for excitement!"

She put her hand on my arm and asked, "Clay, do you *believe* all those stories about yourself? Do you feel that you have to *live up* to them?"

I scoffed at the idea but I am wondering, is it possible?

I do not know. All I know is that I can not go back to what I was. There is only one direction for me and that is forward.

My second book is filled.

BOOK THREE

(1873—1876)

Hays, Kansas, in the year of 1873, was one of the most tremendous "cow towns" on the frontier. Every season, in excess of half a million head of cattle were driven into its shipping yards and more than five thousand cowboys rampaged through its streets.

It was a brutal town, filled beyond capacity with every outcast type of male and female known in the West, all of whom "infested" the massive South Side area—a sprawling conglomerate of saloons, dance and gambling halls, brothels, and honky tonks of all varieties.

It was this notorious zone which was to be Clay's responsibility.

April 4, 1873

Arrived in Hays this morning.

After leaving Anne in the house we are to live in, I was given a ride around the town by a man named Streeter, a member of the City Council.

He showed me the South Side first. It is like the South Main area in Caldwell but about five times as large.

I had to ask Streeter to be shown the North Side of Hays which is beyond the so-called "Dead-line." (The railroad tracks.) This is where all the "respectable" citizens live. I asked Streeter why the house they gave us is not on the North Side and he said that it was on the South Side so that I could be "closer to my work."

The way he said it made it clear that the real reason is that

Anne and I are not considered good enough to live among the "gentry." I did not like his answer but did not make a point of it. I may, later.

As the buggy passed the Sheriff's office, I saw him at the window, glaring out at me. His name is Woodson.

"My rival?" I asked.

Streeter told me that I should not be concerned with Woodson.

"The ones to worry about are the ones who control Woodson," he said.

These are the Griffins who, he says, are nothing less than out and out criminals. Criminals, however, who have learned not only to remain within the "good graces" of the law but, actually, employ it for their own purposes.

They are very wealthy, Streeter told me. The bulk of their riches, he said, comes from cattle rustling and stage coach hold ups! No one has ever succeeded in getting the goods on them however. Any one who tries is soon put out of the way. The Griffin "empire," as Streeter called it, has been "well secured" by threats and violence.

In addition to the rustling and the hold ups, like the Circle Seven, the Griffins control all the usable water sources for miles around and require cattle drovers to pay dearly for its use. On top of that, any cows that happen to stray during these drives are quickly picked up, clumsily rebranded and sold back to their original owners. The owners know that they are being "taken" royally but are in no position to object being far outnumbered by the Griffin forces.

As Streeter told me all those things, I could feel that long lost "tingle" returning. I welcomed it back as I would an old friend. I do not believe that this job is going to be more than I can handle but it promises to be one H——— of a hot one!

Later: After having lunch with Anne, I helped her to unpack.

She seemed a little more resolved to being here. The house is not bad. It is not as nice as her home in Hickman but it is a big improvement over the hotel in Caldwell.

After I had helped her, I took a stroll to the City Marshal's office. There, I met my Deputy, a man named Ben Pickett.

He is a small, quiet man in his forties (I guess) with a straggly mustache and a stocky build. He is not flashy in any way, looking more like a store clerk than a Deputy Marshal. He strikes me, however, as the sort of man who might be out-drawn and outshot but would "get his man" regardless. I took a liking to him and he seems to like me too.

He showed me this week's edition of the *Hays Gazette*. (The editor, he tells me, is another wheel in the Griffin machine.) The headline shocked me, I confess. It reads KILLER MARSHAL ARRIVING! The article goes on to state that "the well-known, cold-blooded pistol killer, Clay Halser, is arriving this week and all citizens of Hays can now look forward to a sanguinary reign of terror."

I must say that it is strange to read these words. While I certainly do not believe all the other kind of articles about me, I have gotten used to being praised. To see the opposite approach puts a fellow back on his heels.

Pickett told me that I should prepare myself for a good deal more of the same. Obviously, he said, the Griffins want me out of the way since I am the only possible fly in their ointment.

Pickett told me, next, about John Harris, a local gambler and saloon owner. Being strictly a "loner," Harris has always opposed the Griffin "regime" and has supported one peace officer after another. He allows them to use his saloon as their "hang out" and spare armory. While expecting no more than token leniency (since, Pickett says, he runs an honest establishment anyway), the value of having the city Marshal as an unofficial ally has been worth, to Harris, ten per cent of the saloon's earnings. Three per cent of this has, by custom, gone to the Deputy Marshal.

Pickett put this to me in a straightforward way and I replied that I was not against the idea if Harris and I got along. I knew that Anne would not object to the prospect of using that seven per cent to build a "nest egg" for the future.

Pickett took me over to the *Keno Saloon* and introduced

me to Harris. He struck me right immediately and agreement was reached. He invited me to take a social drink with him and I said that I would.

When the bar keep brought the bottle to the table, I was delighted to discover that he was none other than Jim Clements!

Harris invited Jim to join us for a drink and we had a nice chat. Harris told me that he has been thinking of approaching various merchants with the idea of "co-sponsoring" a series of prize-fighting matches. Cow boys coming into Hays are always hungry for "diversions," he said. A special entertainment like that could make us all a good raise. He asked me if I would be interested in getting in on it. He said that I would not have to put up any money. My name alone would give the project "stature."

I told him that I would be happy to lend my name to such a venture if it would help. I had a few more drinks with them, then went home, feeling very good. Not only had I met two men who, I believe, promise to make fine friends, but have also gotten together again with Jim. Not to mention the sources of extra income I am finding here.

When I got home, I told Anne that, despite her fears, Hays is going to be the making of us. "We are going to like it here," I said.

As I spoke, there was a thundering of hooves outside and a body of men pulled up in front of the house. In my shirt sleeves, but wearing my Colt in plain sight, I stepped out onto the porch to see who it was.

It was the Griffin family out in force to take a look at Hays' new peace officer—and, I have no doubt, to try to rattle me from the start.

"Just rode in to see the famous Marshal Halser," said a toothless old man. He introduced himself as Roy Griffin, the head of the family. They all sat on their horses "—measuring me."

I thought that it would not hurt to get the jump on them so I said, "That is very kind of you. If you are planning to stay in town, however, you will have to check your weapons at the jail. It is the new rule."

Roy Griffin made a noise that was, I guess, amusement. "Is that right?" he said.

I did not reply but smiled to show him that I was not cowed by him or his sons and brothers.

"Seems as how the *former* Marshal tried to make that same rule," he said. "As long as we are in town, we might as well pay *him* a visit too. He is out on Boot Hill with the other Marshals."

"I intend to stay right here," I told him, trying to sound unconcerned.

"Bless me, sonny, so did they," he answered.

He pulled his horse around and the Griffins rode off in a cloud of dust. I watched them until they had ridden out of sight, then went back inside. Anne had been watching from the window. She did not have to speak. I knew the question in her mind.

We are going to like it here?

Later: It is almost one o'clock in the morning. I have just gotten Anne to bed.

Relieving Pickett at six, I told him that, starting tomorrow, we would begin enforcing the "no guns while in town" policy. I asked him to go to a printer's shop in the morning and have some posters made.

He left and, after a while, I went out on my first rounds.

The South Side, at night, is like a city in H———, I think—all noise and smoke and flickering light. Partly, it excites the senses, partly it repels them.

I walked through it all as though I owned it. It is the only way to demonstrate authority. These kind of people do not recognize anything but a show of strength.

I gave them all the show they expected. I was wearing my best black suit, my best black hat and boots, a good white shirt with a string tie and my brocaded waistcoat; what they call "gambler's dress." I kept my coat unbuttoned so that they could see the butt of my Colt at all times. (I have decided, after some thought, to stick with a .45 even though it is harder to handle.) It has more "stopping" power.

Wherever I went, I knew that they were watching me.

Looking for some sign of weakness. They never saw one. I did not exchange a word with anybody. I merely nodded at people, smiling a little as if the sight of them amused me. No one approached or addressed me.

Until, some hours later, when a gang of cow boys from the Griffin ranch rode in.

Although the "no guns" rule is not to take effect until tomorrow, I decided to "set the stage" by making an example of the Griffins.

I walked quickly to confront them as they were tying up in front of a saloon. I told them that the policy was to surrender their guns when in town and told them that I expected them to obey.

There were nine men in the group. One of them was one of Griffin's sons—I think his name is Jess. He looked at me with a scornful smile and asked if I intended to stand up against all of them.

"If that is what you want," I said.

They did some "tongue skirmishing" with me but I did not back down. Finally, they decided to take off their guns and went into the saloon, leaving their belts slung over a hitching post. As they went inside, they cursed and threatened me under their breath, but I did not object to that as it enabled them to "let out steam."

By that time a crowd had collected and I was glad they had as it gave them the opportunity to see me at work. I dispersed them and they went away.

One of them turned out to be John Harris. He came over and told me that he "admired" how I had handled the cow boys. He did not say so in as many words but I got the feeling that, if the cow boys had tried to resist, Harris would have given me back action.

This impresses me and makes me like him even more. We had a nice chat as he helped me carry the guns and rifles to the jail.

When I got home at midnight, my satisfaction turned to ashes. To my dismay, I found the house dark, its windows shot out and its siding pocked with holes.

I was about to run inside when Pickett came down the street from his house. He told me that Anne and Melanie were safe but that he and his wife had decided that it might be better for her to stay at their house until I had gotten back.

I asked him what had happened and he answered that a group of riders, leaving town, had opened fire on the house. I know d——— well it was Griffin's son and those cow boys.

I went to Pickett's house and got Anne. I told her that no such thing will happen again. She did not argue but I do not think she believes me. The incident really shocked her.

I will see to it that such a thing does *not* happen again. If war is what the Griffins want, I am prepared to give it to them.

Standing back at a distance of time, it is possible to note a thread of what might be termed "over-assurance" running through Clay's entries during this period.

Although he was only one man, he seemed to possess a confidence in his ability which went beyond logic. His standing up to nine men and demanding that they disarm is indicative of this overconfidence.

His writing that he was prepared to declare war on the vast Griffin empire is, while, perhaps, courageous, also somewhat foolhardy.

There seems little doubt that Clay genuinely believed himself to be the equal of any impending situation, however dangerous.

The legend had begun to eclipse the man.

The next edition of the Hays Gazette *described Clay's "brutal treatment" of a "defenseless" group of cowboys. That this group was from the Griffin ranch was not mentioned. Neither was the riddling of Clay's house with his wife and baby daughter inside.*

Clay's wrath at this distorted account was not diminished by the arrival, in town, of one well-shot-up, well-robbed stagecoach.

April 13, 1873

I decided, this morning, that it was time to make a counter move against the Griffins.

Pickett and I rode out to the Griffin ranch, timing our arrival so that they would be at lunch.

Roy Griffin and his brothers and sons came out onto the porch to see what I had to say. I saw their women watching at the windows.

I told them that, from now on, I intend to ride as guard on any stage coach shipment of great value.

I also told them that, if any of them dares to shoot at my house again, I will return the favor without asking permission of the City Council—except that I will use shotguns loaded with scrap iron.

That done, Pickett and I backed our horses away from the house—not from fear so much as a desire to show them how little we thought of them—and rode back to town.

The next move is theirs.

April 19, 1873

Before he left the office tonight, Ben made the suggestion that I reload my revolver daily. He told me that an overnight temperature change, in cooling the gun, can gather moisture in the chambers and cause a misfire.

I have never given it much thought before but I will start to do as he suggests. He made the good point that, considering the hazards of our job, we can not afford the risk of a single bad shot.

I am going on my rounds now.

It is a coincidence that, after writing about the "hazards of our job," I went out and faced one.

Whether it was the "next move" by the Griffins, I do not know. It may have been.

While I was walking past an alley, some one took a shot at me. The lead bit off a corner of my hat brim but did not harm me.

I saw the man running away and started chasing him. After a brief pursuit, I cornered him in a blind alley and, drawing my Colt, ordered him to raise his arms.

I do not think it was bravery so much as panic that made him draw and try to kill me. I wanted to hit him in the leg but there was not time to aim and my instinctive firing took its toll. The man died instantly, a ball entering his body just below the heart.

It was one of Griffin's cow hands.

April 23, 1873

Another lying story in the *Gazette* today. This one tells how "Marshall Clay 'Heroic' Halser" shot down a poor, "unarmed" cowboy after "bullying him unmercifully."

I am trying not to let Bellingham (*the Gazette editor. F.L.*) make me lose my temper. Streeter said that I can not so much as threaten him. I am expected to prove, by "deed," that his words are lies.

I do not know how long I can go along with that. Anne is becoming very upset with the stories. The worst thing is that I am not sure whether she believes me when I tell her that every word is a lie. I guess it is hard to believe that something in print is completely false.

The sentence that bothers her most is: "It becomes more apparent, with each passing day, that Halser has come to believe all the extravagant myths about his Greatness and now regards himself as above the law."

We had some words about that.

"Do you believe it?" I asked.

"No. But . . ."

"But *what?*" I asked. "Either you believe it or you don't. Which is it?"

"I don't know," she said after a while. "I just don't know."

That got my wind up and I replied, "Well, let me know when you make up your mind."

I am feeling hot under the collar as I write this. I still love Anne but, I must say, she seems to think a good deal less of me than I do of her.

I do not believe she has any idea of what it is like to be in my position. On the one hand, I am swamped with printed lies that make me sound like the Second Coming Of The Lord. On the other hand, I am, now, being swamped with printed lies that make me sound like a cross between a rattlesnake, an Apache and Emil Zandt!

Somewhere in between these two extremes I am trying to do my job as City Marshal of Hays . . . but it is not easy. If Anne knew how simple it would be for me to "throw my weight" around, she would be shocked. I could shoot down every man who stood in my way if I chose. I could horse whip that b———— Bellingham and shut him up too!

I am not doing any of these things. I think I am showing considerable patience and wish she could see it.

Later: More trouble.

After I left the house, I went down to the bank and signed contracts which commit me to the prize fight exhibitions. John thinks that we should make a regular thing of them and I agree.

After signing the contracts, he and I went to the *Keno* for a drink.

We were standing at the counter, talking, when a cow boy came in and approached me.

"Halser," he said.

I looked at him. There was no doubt in my mind that he was there for blood.

"My name is Barrett," he said. "It was my friend you murdered."

"I am sorry about that," I said. "It was . . ."

". . . *murder*," he interrupted me. "And I have come to right the wrong."

Here is a good example of what I was writing about before. If I had chosen, I could have drawn on him immediately. Instead I tried to talk Barrett out of it. As calmly as I could, I explained what had happened.

"What you read in the *Gazette* is a lie," I said. "I did not murder your friend. He tried to kill me from ambush and missed. I chased him through the alleys and, when I caught him, I told him to raise his hands. I was going to put him in jail but he drew his revolver and I had no choice but to defend myself. That is God's truth, Barrett, and I hope you will have the good sense to believe it."

I could do no more. As the Lord is my witness, I did the best I could but he would not accept it. He said that he wanted revenge and nothing else would satisfy him.

At last, I gave up trying and we went outside. By then, I had lost my temper and did not care any more. If the man would not back down from me, what was I supposed to do?

We faced each other on the street at a distance of approximately five yards.

"Your play," I told him.

Despite his air of confidence, he fumbled at the crucial moment. As in his friend's case, I would have liked to wound him. It was too late for that however. I can not control my reflexes that late in the game. I put a ball in his chest which passed directly through his heart. He was dead before he landed on the ground.

There is only one thing that disturbs me. (I do not feel guilty for having defended myself.) The man was very quick with his hand. (I learned, after, that he had won eight gun duels previously.) If he had not fumbled, it might have been a close thing.

Is it possible that his fear of my reputation won the battle for me?

Two observations can be made about this entry.

One: Clay seems, for the first time, to be aware of the possibility that his eminence in Hays might not be based entirely on facts.

Two: One might question Clay's presentation of the incident with Barrett. If the two men were standing together at the counter, would it not have been possible for Clay to "buffalo" him and put him in jail, thus sparing his life? Of course, this may have been impractical. Barrett may not have been standing close enough. Further, Clay might have felt that, even if he did buffalo Barrett and put him in jail, it would only be fore-stalling the inevitable "moment of truth" between them.

At any rate, more conflict with Anne ensued because of the killing.

Despite Clay's efforts to convince her that he was justified, the incident drove yet another wedge between them.

Even John Harris coming to tell her what had actually happened did not diminish her reaction.

The situation was aggravated further by a special edition of the Gazette, *the headline of which shrieked WANTON MURDER!*

April 25, 1873

Jim has suggested that I tell Bellingham there will be genuine wanton murder if he does not stop printing lies about me.

I confess that I am giving his suggestion serious thought.

I have never been exposed to any thing like this. It is more than criticism. That d——d Bellingham is out to nail my hide to the wall!

The Council told me again that I must not hurt him though.

They called me in this afternoon to let me know that my "image" is "assuming most unfavorable proportions." (A Rayburn remark if ever I heard one!)

"Is all this killing absolutely necessary?" Mayor Gibbs asked.

"No," I said. "It is not necessary at all. I could let them murder me."

That remark did not win any prizes but I did not care. The way things are in Hays, I figure that they need me a H———— of a lot more than I need them. Surviving Marshals do not grow on trees.

Any way, I told them that they could have my badge back

if they wanted it because I did not plan to continue as peace officer if deprived of the basic right to keep myself alive.

They backed down as I knew they would. Streeter had to have the last word though.

"We *would* appreciate it," he said, "if you would, at least, *endeavor* to keep the peace with more decorum."

"I will certainly try," I answered. "The next time some one tries to kill me, I will slap their wrist and make them stand in the corner."

I left that meeting in a rage. I am beginning to see what a pawn I am in the game between the Council and the Griffins.

When Woodson stopped me in the street, I was just about ready for bear.

He told me that he might have to arrest me for the two shootings!

I looked at him as if he were a tarantula about to crawl up my leg. "You do that," I said. "Any time at all." I unbuttoned my coat. "Why not now?" I suggested.

He backed off, holding his hands away from his body. "There is nothing personal in this, Marshal," he said.

"I would not bet on that hand either," I answered, walking off.

An attempt, the following week, to rob the stagecoach of a valuable gold bullion shipment failed as Clay and Ben Pickett rode as guards.

Clay's unexpected presence inside the coach proved to be the difference. His devastating rifle fire augmenting Pickett's routed the attackers, killing four of them. All were known Griffin employees.

Reprisal came the following night.

May 5, 1873

It is almost three o'clock in the morning. Anne has just fallen asleep. I think that we are safe in Ben's house but I am not taking any chances for a while and will stay awake.

It is fortunate that I am a light sleeper. I woke up about midnight and smelled smoke. Jumping out of bed, I found smoke filling the hall. I woke up Anne and got her and Melanie out the front door before the blaze in the kitchen and hall had reached the stairs.

Then I ran back upstairs and started throwing our clothes out on the roof and then to the ground. Anne hurried to Ben's house and he came down the block and helped me. We got almost all our belongings out. The house could not be saved however. Ben rode to get the volunteer fire fighters but the house was an inferno by the time he rounded them up.

Ben has told us to stay here in their son's room until we find another place. He has been a lot of help tonight and Marion was very comforting to Anne.

After Melanie was asleep, Anne told me that she believes it was a terrible mistake for us to have come here.

"I think we should leave as soon as possible," she said. "We have Melanie's life to consider if not our own."

I tried to be patient with her and assure her that I would settle with the Griffins. (I know they were behind the fire.)

"That would do no good," she said. "There would just be some one else to settle with *you* then. Don't you see that this is more than you can handle?"

I did not care to hear her say that but I did not tell her so. I told her that I had two dependable Deputies (*Clay had persuaded Jim Clements to become his second Deputy. F.L.*) and could handle anything the Griffins chose to throw at me.

"Well, *I can't*," she answered. "I will not be able to sleep a wink now, fearing what they might do to us."

I tried to reassure her but there was no way of doing it. Finally, I had to remind her that I have signed a contract and am bound to respect it.

That made her cry. I put my arms around her and told her that things are not as bad as she imagined. We can find another house, I told her. I reminded her of the money we are going to make—not only from the higher salary and fine commissions but, also, from my percentage of the *Keno* earnings and my twenty per cent of the proceeds from the coming prize fight matches.

None of it helped. She kept crying and saying that Melanie was going to be killed. Finally, to quiet her, I told her that, if things do not settle down by the end of my year here, we will move back East, maybe to Pine Grove. That seemed to satisfy her although she still feels that something awful is going to happen if we do not leave right away.

I know one thing. I am not going back to Pine Grove unless it is in a Pine Box!

May 6, 1873

ell, we are off again.

Anne seemed to settle down a little after last night. Then she saw my journal on the bedroom table and read my last entry.

Now we are further apart than ever. I told her that I only meant that I hate Pine Grove. There are other places we can go, I said. But I think she knows that I do not want to go back East under any condition.

It is just as well she knows it now. She will simply have to learn to accept our life in Hays, that is all. I have a good setup here and am not going to be driven out by those d———d Griffins!

I am sitting on the balcony of the *Hays House* as I write this. I think I had better keep my Record Book in the office from now on.

Down on the stage, men are finishing up preparing the prize fight ring for tonight's match. John is down there with them, telling them what to do.

I have been reading that G——— d———d *Gazette*. Now Bellingham is serializing one of those stupid "novels" about me. He certainly went out of his way to pick the dumbest one he could find! He has added his own bright comments here and there. I do not know how much longer I intend to let him puff. If it were not for the City Council, I would—

* * *

Later: D————, d————, d————and double d————!

While I was writing before, Woodson came in with a summons to stop the match.

They have dug up some d————d city ordinance no body ever heard about which says that it is against the law to conduct "an athletic event" within the city limits. I do not know if it is a real ordinance or something they made up just for the occasion. Naturally, they waited until we had gone to all the trouble of getting things ready before making their move!

John and I are all for going ahead and saying to H————with Woodson, the Griffins and their d————d ordinance. But our "partners" have jelly in their spines and are afraid to tangle with the Griffins so they have run off like a pack of dogs.

The setback is a costly one, especially to John.

Later: After midnight. I have just gotten back from duty.

Another killing. My luck is turning sour, it seems.

Not that I was the one who did the killing but that will not help.

It was after ten o'clock when I stopped at the *Keno* for a drink.

John was playing cards with some men. I had not spoken to him all day because he was in a black mood and I knew that he did not choose to talk. When I came in, he merely nodded his head at me.

As bad luck would have it, one of his opponents was a big cow boy named Ernie. Ernie kept peeking at the discards while they were playing. He was drunk and said that he always did that when he was playing.

John kept telling him again and again to stop monkeying with the dead wood and play cards but Ernie would not listen. He was obviously the kind of man who always goes his own way.

Except for tonight. John got sick of talking to him finally, threw down his cards and raked in the pot (he and Ernie were the only ones left in the hand), telling Ernie to get out of his saloon.

Ernie got mad and demanded his money back. When John told him to go to H————, Ernie pulled a knife on him.

It all happened too fast for me to stop it. (I was across the room at the counter.) I have never seen John in action before. If he pulls a gun like he does a knife, I am certainly glad he is on my side. In a split second, he had thrown the blade into Ernie's chest.

We took Ernie to Doc Warner's place but he died a few minutes after we arrived.

This comes at a bad time. Still I do not see what else John could have done. He was in the right about the game and in the right about defending himself.

Still, knowing Bellingham, I suspect that John's association with me will not be overlooked.

Clay's suspicion proved a sound one.

What he did not foresee was that Bellingham, preferring Clay as his main target, put as much blame on him as on Harris.

HALSER SUPPORTS MURDER! was the headline, the story going on to say that "with sneering defiance of lawful procedure" Clay was permitting "one of his cronies, the notorious gambler-killer, John Harris, to go scot free after having cold-bloodedly knifed to death an un-armed, law-abiding" cowboy.

Clay's temper proved his master on this occasion—although its outcome proved more confusing than satisfying to him.

May 10, 1873

I went to see Bellingham before.

"Come to add me to your list of murders, have you?" was the first thing he said to me. He said it almost before I had shut the door to his office.

"I have not murdered any one and you know it," I said, taking his words at face value.

"I do *not* know it," he replied. "On the contrary, I know

that you *have* committed murder and will doubtless do so again."

"If I do," I told him, "you are number one on the list."

"Good!" he cried. "That is my badge of honor!"

"You had better stop printing lies about me or you will be sorry," I said.

"That's it!" he said. "Threaten me! That is your way, isn't it?"

I swear to God I could not get through to him. I think he is loco. If he is afraid of me, he is certainly good at hiding it. I have a feeling that he *hopes* I will kill him!

I have never run across a man like him before. One thing is certain though. If he is not afraid of dying, threatening his life is a waste of time. Worse than a waste of time. The idea seems to thrill him!

I left the *Gazette* office in a stew. I am disgusted that it turned out that way. My only consolation is that Bellingham is crazy and the words of a crazy man are not as bothersome as those of a sane man.

While I was walking back to the office to see Jim, I met Streeter. He told me that the City Council wants me to break off with John.

I told him that, if there is ever a show down with the Griffins, there are only three men in this whole d———d town I can depend on and as one of these is John Harris, I intend to remain in contact with him.

I did not bother telling him that I like John and that John is my friend. He would not have understood.

Later: That d———d crazy Bellingham has come out with a special one sheet edition of the *Gazette*, the whole thing devoted to a story about how I "bullied" my way into his office and threatened his "life and limb." "Nonetheless," writes courageous Mr. Bellingham, "so long as blood shall flow in my veins and breath in my lungs, I shall continue to espouse the cause of truth and justice though it may mean my very existence!"

I am sure now that he would love to be killed. I am also beginning to wonder if the Griffins really do pay him off. If they do, they are wasting their money. I think Bellingham would do it for nothing!

I guess I will have to learn to live with his *Gazette*.

I told Anne about my visit to Bellingham but I do not think she believes a word I say any more. Our life together has become nearly intolerable. I have not touched her for more than a month.

All she says to me these days is that she wants to leave Hays and that, if we don't leave right away, something terrible is going to happen.

Later: Past one o'clock in the morning.

Almost "cashed in" tonight.

While I was walking my rounds, eighteen cow hands from the Griffin Ranch galloped into town and started shooting up Main Street.

I was too far from the office to get there fast so I started for the *Keno* to pick up a shotgun.

I was running down the alley when three of the cow hands pulled up behind me and ordered me to stop.

I turned to face them. They had me dead to rights, all three of them pointing their revolvers at me.

"Why don't you draw, Marshal?" said one of them.

"Yeah, Marshal, why don't you draw?" said another. "You are so all-fired fast."

"Go ahead," said the third. "Fill your hand. You are the Great Marshal Halser, aren't you? You should be able to get the drop on us, you are so fast."

I knew that I would probably be killed but I was getting ready to take a crack at it when, fortunately, the play was turned. John heard the cow hands' voices through a window inside the *Keno*, grabbed a sawed off shotgun and crashed it through the window, pointing it at the three men.

"All right," he said. "Marshal Halser is ready now. Commence to firing."

Seeing him at the window with that shotgun pointing at them took the wind out of their sails. They dropped their irons and, while John marched them to jail, I took the shot-gun and started after the other cow boys.

There is nothing like a few good blasts from a sawed off shotgun to clear a street. I did not even have to shoot any of them.

I owe my life to John now. And Streeter wants me to break off with him!

When I got home, Anne was still awake.

"So you are back," she said.

"What do you mean?" I asked.

"I heard the shooting," she said. "I thought they would be bringing your body home on a board."

"It was nothing," I told her.

I hope she does not hear what happened.

Clay's hope was groundless. Not only did Anne learn what happened but other occurrences began to happen as well.

Clandestine attempts on his life—and, to a lesser degree, on the lives of Pickett, Clements, and Harris—picked up tempo steadily.

It was a rare night when, making his rounds, Clay failed to hear lead whistling by him in the darkness, followed by the sound of running feet and/or the hoofbeats of a galloping horse.

He began avoiding bright lights and dark alleys and took to walking in the middle of the street. He seriously considered Jim Clements' suggestion that he make his rounds on horse-back in order to present a poorer target.

He entered buildings by shoving open doors with the barrel of the sawed off shotgun he always carried now, then sliding in quickly to place his back to the wall.

He began to wear a second .45 caliber Colt revolver at his right hip. He purchased a pair of Derringers and carried them in his waistcoat pockets. He was a walking arsenal while on his rounds, prepared to deal with any and all emergencies. He was never again "caught short" as he had been outside the Keno Saloon *that night.*

Day by day, his state of tension mounted. While not actu-

ally afraid (his entries make this clear) he did become increasingly nervous until unexpected noises made him jump and minor irritations evoked responses far beyond their due. (His relationship with Anne reached its nadir during this period and several entries indicate that he began "taking up" with one of the dance hall girls.)

His appetite decreased and he began to lose weight. He had difficulty sleeping. His face became haggard and lined. All in all, he was a far cry from the lighthearted young man who had traveled West with such eagerness seven years earlier.

The legend had begun to take its toll.

August 20, 1873

This evening started bad and got worse.

While I was preparing to go on shift, Anne watched me in silence as I put the two reloaded Derringers into my waistcoat pockets and buckled on my pair of reloaded revolvers.

When I started reloading the sawed off shotgun, she exploded.

"Look at you!" she cried. "You are a one man Army! How long is this going to go on?"

I did not try to pacify her. I have given up on that. "I want to stay alive," was all I said.

"Then leave Hays!" she cried.

"I have a job," I said.

"Then *quit* the job!"

We went on like that for quite a while but nothing new was said.

Then, as I started walking her (and Melanie) down the block so she could pay a visit to Marion, a young fellow who had been waiting in the street blocked our way.

He could not have been more than sixteen, a skinny, mean-faced kid wearing a revolver. I almost knew what he was going to say before he opened his mouth.

"Are you Clay Halser?" he asked.

"Get out of the way," I told him.

"I hear that you are fast with a gun," he said.

My patience is not much to speak of these days. "*Get out of the way*, I said," I told him. "Can't you see I have my wife and child with me?"

That got his back up.

"Are you hiding behind your wife's skirts?" he replied.

"For the last time," I told him, "*get out of the way.*"

"Not until I get my satisfaction," he said. "I have come a long way to meet you and will not be denied."

I had to restrain myself from killing him that instant.

"Go on ahead," I said to Anne.

"Clay," she began.

"Go on ahead," I interrupted her.

"Clay, don't do this," she begged.

"I said, go *on.*" I took her by the arm and started her off. She gasped at the grip of my hand, then, without another word, started for Ben's house, crying and not looking back.

Just then Ben came running down the plank walk with a shotgun in his hands.

"All right, drop your gun belt," he told the boy.

The boy smiled with contempt. "Well," he said to me, "no wonder you have lasted so long. You have so much help."

I was almost shaking with rage by then. The expression on his face finished it.

"Go back," I told Ben.

"Clay, let me put him in jail until he cools off," he said.

"*Go back!*" I yelled at him.

He started to say something more, then saw the look on my face and turned away. After he had walked some yards, I spoke to the boy.

"All right, you loud mouth, son of a b——," I said. "You want to try me, go ahead."

His face got tight. "Draw," he said.

"I don't have to draw," I told him. "I can wait. You haven't got a chance in H———."

He didn't either. He went for his revolver but never got it out. I have never been so fast. Before he could clear half his scabbard I had put two balls through his heart. He was dead before he started to fall.

I left him in the street and walked away. As I passed Ben's house I could see Anne looking at me.

I am sick and tired of that look! You would think I am a common murderer.

While scarcely a common murderer, it does seem apparent that Clay had, by this time, reached the point where immediate killing was preferable to extended arguments. Completely confident in his ability to handle any armed opponent, he had lost the patience to deal with them in any other way than instant action. Like his guns, he was always "cocked and ready."

He no longer cared about the stories in the Gazette. *He paid no attention to the castigations of the City Council. He openly defied the Griffins to do their worst.*

Reports from other sources at this time confirm the fact that he had become almost brutal in his attitudes.

He was not surprised or even much disturbed when Anne decided to leave.

September 5, 1873

Anne is leaving.

She says that she can not go on living this way.

She says that she does not feel as though she knows me any more.

She says that I could have put that boy in jail if I had wanted to but that it was "easier" for me to kill him.

She says that she is going to Hickman to live with her aunt.

She says that she wants me to go with her but I think she is saying it because she feels it is the thing to do. When I reminded her that I have a contract to respect, she did not argue the point.

She says that she will expect me after my contract expires but I think she knows I will not be showing up.

My feelings about her leaving are mixed ones.

It does not do my "image" any good to have my wife "walk out" on me. I can tell people that she is leaving for some other reason but every one will know the real reason. That part I do not like.

At the same time, I feel as if a weight is being lifted off my back. I love Melanie and will miss her but my life with Anne has become a trial. There is nothing left between us. She does not respect me any more or believe in what I am doing.

It is just as well that she leaves.

Following Anne's departure, Clay began to manifest, even more, the acid temperament which Marshal Hickok had vented on him years before.

He understood that temperament now. The strain of remaining alert for violence which could erupt at any moment of the day or night was wearing him thin.

He installed a bolt on the door of the hotel room into which he had moved.

He never went to sleep without placing crumpled newspaper pages at strategic places on the floor, most of them around the door and window despite the bolt and the fact that the window overlooked a drop of more than twenty feet.

He kept a weapon within easy reach at all times, sleeping with his gunbelt hung across the head board of the bed, a Derringer beneath the pillow.

He held a revolver in his hand when being shaved, concealing it beneath the barber's cloth, his eyes fixed on the wall mirror so that he could keep the doorway under constant observation.

He kept his right hand free at all times, even training himself to use a fork with his left.

He always sat with his back to the wall.

The need to remain ready for action, whether awake or asleep, drained him steadily. Jumpy and in constant need of rest, he began drinking more than usual.

An indication of his mental state is provided by the following entry.

October 27, 1873

Found out tonight exactly what those G——— d——d people on the North Side think of me.

A bunch of drunken cow boys started firing their guns as they were leaving town. That was all right with me. They do it all the time. It is a way for them to let off steam that hurts no body.

Then they rode into the North Side doing it and woke up the people. I rode after them and chased them out.

After they were gone, I saw the people at their windows and standing on their porches.

Not one of them addressed a word to me. They looked at me as if I was no better than the cow boys. No one asked me to chase after them but I did. Now these people looked at me as if I was a hound that had gotten out of the dog house. I almost fired my shotgun into the·air to shake them up, they made me so mad. I didn't though. I touched the brim of my hat like a good Marshal should do and rode away.

B——s! I am their hired gun, no more! The strong right arm of the D———merchants! They don't care about law and order! All they care about is making their "pound of flesh" in peace and quiet!

Clay's next problem came from an old source. F.L.

November 5, 1873

Henry Blackstone showed up today. He is staying at the hotel and tells me that he plans to pay me a "nice, long visit."

It is not bad to see him again but I do not have the same feeling about him I had before.

We are just not cut out of the same cloth. He is loyal to his friends, I suppose, but that is all he is loyal to. He had no reason to leave Hickman, it turns out. He had just gotten "bored" with me gone and had decided to "go find some excitement."

He is just not my sort as Jim and Ben and John are. He still looks the same too! It is unbelievable! When I look in the mirror, I see my years and more. But Henry does not look a day older. There is certainly something to be said for not taking anything seriously.

He still smiles all the time and my friends are taken with him. I do not imagine there is any reason to warn them about him. Since they are my friends, Henry will not do anything to harm them.

Still, I wish he was not here at this time. I have enough problems. He hinted that he would not mind being a Deputy and "helping me out" again but I told him that I had two Deputies and did not need any more. That is a lie. I could use *ten* good Deputies. *Good* Deputies though.

I am not sure, any more, that I could depend on Henry in a real tight.

I hope to G———— he behaves himself.

As the foregoing entry makes clear, Clay's attitude toward Blackstone had undergone almost a complete reversal.

Whether this was based on genuine awareness of Blackstone's potentially dangerous amorality or simply on resentment that time had treated his old friend so easily can not be known. Probably, it was a combination of the two. Clay had been through many harrowing experiences since he had last seen Blackstone. He was simply not the same man Blackstone had known.

Since Blackstone (if we are to accept Clay's word) was ex-actly the same person as he had always been, there would, inevitably, have been no ground for a relationship between them anymore.

Several weeks passed during which Blackstone "behaved" himself. Clay began to feel a little more at ease with his old comrade although he never did manage to achieve the camaraderie they had once enjoyed together. He played cards and drank with Blackstone, spent considerable time with him, reminiscing.

Without mentioning, again, the idea of him being a Deputy,

Henry made himself useful to Clay, Pickett and Clements, re-
lieving them off and on to give them more free time. In his al-
most childlike way, Blackstone was, perhaps, trying to "earn
back" Clay's approval so that he could, once more, be Clay's
Deputy.

Then, when Clay was actually considering the possibility,
Blackstone altered everything.

November 21, 1873

Well, I am in the soup again with the Council, Bellingham,
and every one who has heard what happened.

I have no excuse this time. I can not hold myself blameless
because Henry is my friend.

I do not know what to do, I have Henry here in jail but, obviously, I can not keep him here because I owe him my life.
Still, when I let him go, there has got to be an outcry heard
from here to Texas.

It happened about an hour ago.

Henry was here with Ben, keeping him company. I was
sleeping in my room.

Ben indicated his desire for a cup of coffee and Henry told
him to go and get one. He said that he would "mind" the office while Ben was gone.

Since every thing was peaceful, Ben accepted the offer and
walked down the street to *Nell's Cafe.*

While he was having his coffee, a group of cow boys rode
in. They had been on the trail a long time and were in no mood
to "be trifled with," a witness later told me. (Ned Young from
the feed store.)

Henry went outside with a shotgun and waved the cow
boys over to the office where he told them that the policy was
to leave their guns at the jail while they were in town.

The cow boys had never been to Hays before and did not
cotton to the idea. One of them was particularly against it . . .
and against Henry for suggesting it. Mistaking Henry's smile
for weakness, he spoke more angrily by the moment.

He was in the middle of an insult when Henry (still smiling, Young said!) blasted him off his saddle with both barrels.

The noise woke me up and I ran to the window of my room. Seeing a crowd collecting outside the jail, I dressed as fast as I could and rushed down stairs.

By the time I got there, Ben was trying to calm the now disarmed cow boys who were in a lynching mood because of what Henry had done.

To quiet them down, I pretended to arrest Henry and put him in jail. That seemed to satisfy them and they rode away, although I have a feeling that the matter is not closed with them.

I put Henry in a cell, leaving the door open. He sat down on the cot and looked at me.

"For G——'s sake, Henry, why did you do it?" I asked.

Henry smiled.

"He was dirty talking me," he answered.

Later: Almost midnight.

Henry is gone.

I was making my rounds when the same group of cow boys rode into town and stopped in front of the office. I went over to talk to them and they told me that they were in for Henry's hide.

I told them that the law would take care of him and, after a while, they left. I knew they would be back after they had had a few drinks though and I moved Henry to my hotel room, using the back door of the jail to get him out.

Shortly after, the cow boys started gathering outside the jail again, this time with a rope in their hands. I knew that, sooner or later, they would find out that Henry was not in the jail so I got Henry's horse and brought it up behind the hotel. I went up and got him down a back staircase and saw him mounted.

"Thanks, old fellow," he said with a smile. "We are even now."

I am glad he realizes that and hope he does not come back any more. I shook his hand and wished him luck but I do not

want to see his face again. He is pure trouble and I have
enough of that already. I should have told him to stay out of
Hays but I did not have the heart.

I just hope that I have seen the last of him.

*Blackstone's departure, while relieving Clay of concern
about his strange, young friend, did not, in any other way, diminish the tension of his demanding schedule.*

*Seven nights a week, from the hours of six o'clock to one in
the morning, he stood duty as City Marshal.*

*He continued riding guard on all valuable stage shipments,
thus completely cutting off this source of the Griffins' income.*

*He had to live with the mounting disfavor of the City Coun-
cil and the North Side populace. Even the men and women of
the South Side disapproved of his releasing Henry. (No one believed his story that Henry had "escaped," least of all Bellingham, who was in his glory with a florid account of "this new
nadir of perfidy" committed by Clay.)*

*Finally, Clay had to continue living under the day-by-day,
hour-by-hour, minute-by-minute strain of knowing that the
Griffins wanted him dead and would continue "working" on
that problem as long as he remained as peace officer.*

*About this time, another problem cropped up, Henry's dis-
appearance strangely paralleled by the re-appearance of an
old acquaintance.*

December 2, 1873

I was having a drink in the *Keno* tonight when a man came
dashing in and said that a cow boy had run amuck in *The Yellow Mandarin (one of Hays's largest brothels. F.L.),* killed
one of the girls, wounded two others, and barricaded himself
in their room, threatening to kill any one who entered.

I hurried over to *The Yellow Mandarin* where a crowd was
waiting downstairs. The room the cow boy was barricaded in
was on the second floor in the rear. I went upstairs and started
down the hall.

As soon as the cow boy heard my footsteps, he fired a shot through the thin door, shattering the wood. I jumped to one side and missed getting hit.

I removed my boots and edged along the wall, revolver in hand. I pressed myself against the wall outside the room and told the cow boy to come out with his hands up or he was a dead man.

"This is Marshal Halser," I told him, "and this is your last chance to come out alive."

"You will have to take me as a corpse!" he shouted.

"Are you going to let those two girls die as well?" I asked.

"I do not care about them!" he shouted. "They are just a couple of w——s!"

I asked him a few more times to surrender, then fired some shots through the door. He fired three shots back, then was quiet. I took the chance that he was reloading and kicked in the door.

That was almost my undoing. Only the shock of seeing me charging in kept him from killing me, I think. He had a Derringer in his hand but his arm jerked when I came in and he missed me by a hair, knocking off my hat. I answered his fire without thought and hit him in the chest, killing him almost instantly.

Then I put my revolver away and checked the girls. The first one I looked at had died from loss of blood.

The second one was not dead. She was not a girl either.

It was Mary McConnell, Anne's stepmother.

Later: Mary McConnell is going to live, Doc Warner says. I have put her in a room at the hotel.

I do not know whether to involve myself with her or turn my back.

I do not owe her any thing but I feel that she needs a hand right now.

She looks terrible. She has lost a power of weight and has little left of the looks she had when I first met her in Hickman.

I do not know how long she has been here in Hays. She

must have known that I was here. Maybe she figured that in a place as big as the South Side, our trails would never cross.

Now they have crossed though and I feel sorry for her. Even if she is only Anne's step mother, I feel as if there is a family tie. Anne went a good distance out of her way to help her once.

I suppose I can go a little way out of mine to do the same.

December 3, 1873

I spoke to Ben and Marion this afternoon and they told me that Mary McConnell is welcome to live in the small shed behind their house while she is recovering. It is nothing fancy but it is clean and Mary has no place else to stay. G——— knows *The Yellow Mandarin* does not want her and I can not afford to keep her at the hotel.

I will speak to Mary McConnell about it tomorrow morning when she wakes up.

As indicated earlier, the purpose of this volume is to convey, via choice selections from Clay Halser's journal, the unfolding of a phenomenon of these, our violent times: namely, the so-called gunfighter and/or lawman.

If one chose to deviate from this avowed intent, one could (as in the case of Clay's courtship of Anne McConnell) expend considerable space to the relationship between Mary McConnell and Jim Clements.

Indeed, an entire, tragic tale emerges from Clay's journal during this period. While not directly involved, he was close enough to the situation to view it with an acute eye and, while the bulk of his entries continued to concern themselves with his own problems as City Marshal of Hays, he did write many an extended paragraph on the McConnell-Clements liaison.

While Mary McConnell was recovering from the wound she had suffered at the hands of the cowboy in The Yellow Mandarin, *Ben and Marion Pickett behaved toward her with the very essence of that much abused word "Christianity."*

In the beginning, Mrs. Pickett brought meals to the shed and fed the injured woman by hand; bathed her, changed her bedclothes and her clothing. When Mary McConnell had recovered enough to care for herself, the Picketts invited her to share their meals in the main house.

It is, hopefully, not amiss at this point to comment briefly on the Picketts. Despite the more sensational aspects of Clay's life, and the lives of men like him, if we are to recognize the truth of the matter, it is people like the Picketts who are the true backbone of social development in the West. Undoubtedly, men like Clay Halser fulfill a definite need. Still, it is the strain of people represented by the Picketts which truly "tames" a town.

Excluding the fact that Ben Pickett was a Deputy Marshal— a somewhat exotic profession even for that time—his attitudes and those of his wife and their day-by-day behavior proved them to be the type which, in the long run, settles wildernesses and creates progress in barren lands.

It is also evident, by these facts, that Clay, despite his faults, had good taste in friends. Ben Pickett, as indicated, was a solid, stable individual. John Harris, despite his background and profession, was known to be an honest man with a straight-forward, dependable nature. Finally, Jim Clements, for all the rough-hewn simplicity of his moral standards, was fundamentally a kindhearted, generous person.

It was, perhaps, his kindness and generosity which led to his relationship with Mary McConnell. Then again, it may have been no more complicated than the loneliness of a man approaching his forties who feels the need of a permanent female companion.

Whatever the cause, when Clements—stopping by the Picketts' house for a visit one afternoon—was introduced to Mary McConnell, the "die was cast."

Before Clay learned of it, Clements was visiting the Pickett house regularly and developing a warm emotion for Mary McConnell who, in turn, was developing a warm emotion for him. On her part, it may well have been the first genuine feeling she had ever experienced. On the other hand, it may have been a move prompted by desperation as, six years his senior and well on her way toward becoming one of the "dregs" of society, she saw, in Clements, a last chance for regeneration.

When Clay discovered what was going on, he tried, without divulging Mary McConnell's unseemly background, to discourage Clements from considering her as more than a friend. This proved of no avail. For the first time, there was friction between the two men and, seeing that his friend was firm in his intention, Clay backed off, not feeling justified in interfering beyond a certain point.

When Clements and Mary McConnell announced their wedding plans, Clay could do no more than hope for the best. Using the Griffins as an excuse, he tried to suggest, to Clements, that he and his bride-to-be leave Hays and make a "fresh start" elsewhere. When this did not work either, he gave up trying and, as his final entry before the wedding states, "crossed my fingers hard."

January 12, 1874

The wedding took place this afternoon, Mary is now Mrs. Clements and I hope to G——— it works out for them. I have never seen Jim so happy. He has always been a quiet, almost not-speaking kind of man who, maybe, cracked a small grin once in a long while.

Today he was all smiles and like a different person.

Thank G———, I was able to keep him that way. After the ceremony, while Jim and Mary were accepting congratulations and well wishes inside the church, I went out to get the buggy so they could drive to their new house.

A couple of South Side men were riding by and stopped to watch as the wedding guests came out. When the men saw Mary, one of them said, "Holy C———, that is Mary from *The Yellow Mandarin*!" He was drunk and I heard him say that he was going to ask her how things were at the w——— house! He got off his horse to do so.

Just before Jim and Mary reached the buggy, I stepped behind the man, pulled a Derringer from beneath my coat and jammed it into his back.

"You say one word and it will be your last," I told him.

He turned into a statue and was as quiet as one as Jim and Mary got into the buggy. Whether or not Mary recognized him, I do not know. She did not seem to.

Any way, we all waved goodbye to them and they departed happily. After they were gone, I put the Derringer away. "If I hear about this any where," I told the man, "I will know who started the talk and come gunning for you."

The man swore on his mother's grave that he would never utter a word. I hope to G———— he does not. I really have got to get Jim and Mary out of Hays somehow. It is just too tight a situation. If Jim found out, I do not know what he would do.

Later: After the party at Jim and Mary's house was over, I went back to the hotel to take a nap before going on duty.

As I neared my room, I saw a figure standing by the door and snatched out my gun.

"Don't shoot," the figure said in a weak voice.

It was Henry. He is very sick and may have pneumonia.

I could not very well turn him away so I helped him to take off his clothes and get into bed. I have never seen his body before. It is covered with scars of every sort, souvenirs from his many knife and gun fights in the past.

He seems quite unlike the Henry I have known. He tries to smile but can not do it too well. He has a terrible cough and can not speak too clearly. All I could make out of what he was saying was that no one saw him come into town and if I will only let him stay a while until he feels a little better, he will never bother me again. The only reason I got that was that he kept on saying it over and over until I understood.

I got Doc Warner and brought him to the room. He said that Henry probably had pneumonia. He gave Henry some medicine and said that he has to stay in bed and keep warm. He is coming back in the morning to check Henry.

I had to leave while I was on duty but I checked Henry

every hour or so and he seemed to remain asleep. He must be exhausted. He does not look like a young man now. He looks like an old man with a young face. His skin is almost grey.

I guess I will have to sleep on the floor tonight. I do not want to leave him. Neither do I want to sleep in a room without a bolt on the door.

I am sitting in the chair, writing this. Henry is still asleep. I feel sorry for him. I have never seen him like this. I never realized how slight of build he is. He has lost considerable weight and, between that and that old-young face of his, he looks terrible lying on the bed.

How can such a pitiful looking creature be such a cold-blooded murderer? It is hard to understand. But then a lot of things are hard to understand. Life is not the simple thing I once believed it to be.

The thing which is most confusing of all to me is how I got to where I am. Was it all just an accident? A coincidence? As I look back, it seems that all the events of my life have combined to make me what I am.

Still, there are others like me who are as fast with a gun and have been Marshals. Why were articles and stories not written about them? Hickok is the only other man I know of who may be in the same position. *Why were we picked out?* Was it an accident? A coincidence?

I wish I knew.

Something about the marriage between Clements and Mary McConnell plus his old comrade showing up so terribly ill seems to have compelled Clay, for the first time, to try and understand the circumstances which had befallen him.

That this frame of mind remained with him for more than a matter of hours is demonstrated by the following entry made six days later.

January 18, 1874

Henry is feeling well enough to sit up. I have almost had to rope him to the bed to keep him down. He keeps saying that he would like to go out and have a drink and a game of cards.

Finally, I had to tell him straight out that he could not go out under any circumstances because of what happened the last time he was here.

"I am in enough trouble already," I told him. *"Don't make any more for me."*

Henry smiled and I was shocked to see a trembling of his lips when he did. "Sure, old fellow," he said. "I do not want to make trouble for you. You are the only friend I have."

That made me feel like a low down skunk although I did not know how to tell him so. I told him that I would bring a deck of cards and some whiskey to the room later and we would have a drink and a game.

Later: It is almost three o'clock in the morning.

I should not have brought the whiskey, I suppose, although Henry did seem to enjoy it despite the coughing. We both drank too much.

He is asleep now. We had a game of cards and he seemed to enjoy that too. He is so much like a child that it is strange to me. I feel like his father now, in some ways. It is impossible for me to believe that once we H——d it up along the border. It seems as if it happened (if it happened at all!) a hundred years ago.

I think I got more good out of tonight than Henry did. After I had had too many drinks, I spent more time "unburdening" myself than playing cards. I do not know why I did it with Henry except that, really, he is the only one I *could* unburden myself to. Ben and John and Jim are all so strong. If I revealed what I felt to them, they would lose their respect for me.

Any way, the more I talked to Henry, the more loose my tongue got until I could not shut up. Henry listened patiently, nodding his head and smiling like he does. I do not know if he really understands what I feel but, at least, he gave me a good ear for the time I spoke.

I told him that, during the Brady-Courtwright War, I sometimes felt as though I was not a person but a part of a machine. I turned and moved but it was all within the confines of the "mechanism" that controlled me.

In Caldwell, I felt it even more.

Now, here in Hays, the feeling has reached its apex. It is as if the conflict between the Griffins and the Council is a chess game. In between the two forces is a pawn standing in the open, right in the middle and way out in front. That pawn is me and all I can do is wait for some Great Hand to move me to the next position where I may live or die.

"You are not a piece on a chess board," Henry told me when I was finished. "You are a man and can do what you want."

For a moment there, something "sparked" between us. Something that was deeper and stronger than any thing we had ever known in the old days. I do not know what it was and it did not last for more than a second or two.

Henry broke it when he smiled and said, "Don't let them ruffle you, old fellow. If they stand in your way, shoot them down."

During Blackstone's period of recovery, Clay received a letter from Anne which multiplied, by many times, his darkened mental state.

She told him that Melanie had fallen down a flight of stairs and almost died. She had recovered but was in such a terribly weakened condition that Anne did not dare to leave her for a moment. Accordingly, she had been unable to look for work to help support the child. Since her aunt was not well off to begin with, what little savings she had possessed had gone to medical expenses for the child, and they were in consequent dire need of funds.

Clay sent whatever money he had on hand, which was not much since Anne had taken all their savings when she left. Newly ridden by a sense of guilt, Clay, in his journal entries, pondered endlessly on what to do. Harris was the only one he knew with any kind of money but he did not feel justified in asking him for a loan, the collapse of the prize fight venture having cost the gambler a large sum. Pickett and Clements were worse off financially than he was. Consequently, all he could do was send whatever portion of his earnings he did not actually need to live on and hope that it was sufficient.

It was not. Anne wrote him constantly, making it clear that the amounts he was sending were not enough to cover her modest cost of living plus the continuing medical expenses for Melanie. There was even the possibility, she wrote, that the child might have to be placed in a hospital for extensive surgery. This, added to Clay's other problems, proved a harrowing blow to his frame of mind.

He was at a peak of inner turmoil when Henry, well and restless, turned the situation into total nightmare.

February 16, 1874

Sweet G————, is there no end to it? Henry has done it *again*!

While I was sleeping this morning, he "got bored" (says his note) and, in spite of everything I have told him, left the room and went to the *Maverick Saloon* for a "drink or two and a quiet game of cards."

With Henry there is no such thing as a quiet anything. I do not know if Galwell was as bad as some say. The few times I have come across him he seemed a little arrogant but no more than a lot of young men whose fathers have money.

I do not know. Maybe he was like Menlo but I doubt it. All I know for certain is that, when he started losing money to Henry, he got mad and made a few remarks.

Shortly after, he paid for that mistake with a bullet in his brain.

Henry has fled. I do not know where he is and care less. I *told* him not to leave the room! "Sure, old fellow. I do not want to make trouble for you. You are the only friend I have." *Sure!*

Galwell's father has offered a reward of a thousand dollars for Henry's capture. Right now, I think I would collect it if I could. I am in the dog house with every body. Henry was recognized as the one who "escaped" from jail that other time. Now every one thinks I let him "escape" again. I can look forward to a blast from Bellingham, several from the City Council and a lot of trouble from the South Siders.

D——— Henry! Why did he have to do it? *What is the matter with him any way?*

Later: I have just heard from Henry.

He sent a note to me by a Mexican sheep herder. He is hiding in the Mexican's shack a few miles out of town and needs a horse. He wants me to bring him one and says that he will never bother me again after today.

Later: it is almost ten o'clock.

I have put Henry in jail.

I never saw such a startled look in my life as that on his face when I pulled my gun and told him he was under arrest. He thought that I was joshing him at first. When he saw that I was not, he never said another word.

He is going to have to stand trial for murder. I can not back him up any more. I paid off my debt to him and we are even. I just can not let him go. He is a cold-blooded killer and must be punished.

I am sending the reward money to Anne to use for Melanie. I suppose that, now, every one will accuse me of "selling" my friend for money. Let them think it if they choose. I am the City Marshal and Henry has broken the law. There is no question about it at all. It was out and out murder.

Galwell was not even armed.

The trial of Henry Blackstone was a brief one. The jury found him guilty of murder and he was sentenced to be hanged.

March 5, 1874

I am writing this in the office. I do not know if I have done the right thing or not. I feel that I have but I am not sure. Is there any way to be sure?

It happened about an hour ago.

It is a cold, rainy day so I brought Henry a good, hot meal from *Nell's Cafe*—soup, and steak, and bread, and pie, and coffee.

When I brought it to the cell and opened the door, Henry smiled.

"Will you sit and jaw with me while I eat?" he asked.

I did not see any harm in it. He seemed calm to me. As he ate, he spoke of different things, mostly his family.

"I hope you will write my Mother," he said to me. "I hate that she should learn I met my end this way but I want her to know. Tell her all that happened. Do not leave out anything."

He talked and talked as he ate. He said he was resigned to his fate and hoped that all the bad talk about him would cease when he had paid his debt and was hanging by a rope, his "soul flung to eternity."

"There has got to be a law," he said. "I see that now. The world would be barbaric if every young fellow lived like me. Now, as the gallows stares me in the face, I recognize what a poor wretch of a person I really am."

I never suspected a thing until, in the middle of a word, he smashed me suddenly across the head with his tray and lunged from the cell.

Dazed, I struggled to my feet and staggered after him. Henry ran outside and started down the plank walk.

If it had not been raining so hard, he might have made it. He started to run across the street to grab a horse that was tied in front of the General Store. He was half way across when he slipped and sprained his leg.

By the time he had limped to the horse and gotten on, I had reached him. I grabbed him by the leg and pulled him off. He fought me like a wildcat but has not recovered from his illness yet and was too weak to beat me. Finally, I got his left arm twisted up behind his back and stuck a gun against his ribs.

It is the only time I ever saw Henry lose control.

"What are you doing?" he cried. "Why don't you let me go?"

I did not answer him which only got him more excited.

"I understand about the reward money!" he cried. "I know you needed it for your baby! But you have *sent* it now! They can not take it back! And no one can blame you if I escape by force!"

I did not answer him. I was still dizzy but also angry that he had pulled such a mean trick on me.

"Clay, I could have killed you if I had wanted to!" he cried. "Don't you see that? *I could have killed you if I had wanted to!*"

He kept saying that over and over as I locked him into his cell. He could not seem to understand why I had not let him escape.

I do not understand it myself.

What made me chase him like that? It would have been simple to let him escape. There would have been an outcry but, soon enough, it would have passed.

Why didn't I let him go then? I know he is a criminal and a murderer and it is my job to keep him under lock and key until he is punished for his crime.

Still, he is *Henry*.

I can see why he does not understand me.

I do not understand myself.

March 9, 1874

This morning came, a desolate one.

Days of rain had ended but the sky was dark and there was a heaviness in the air.

Henry was sitting in his cell, smoking a cigar, when Ben and I went to get him. He had eaten every scrap of the breakfast we had brought to him—steak, and eggs, and coffee, and apple pie.

"I have been listening, for days, to the work men building that contraption out there," he told us with a smile. "I sure have wondered what it looks like. I am glad I am going to see before I die of curiosity."

I could barely speak. I had been up all night and had nothing in my stomach because I felt sick.

"I am sorry," I said, holding up the shackles and chain. "We have to put this on you."

"Oh, that is all right," Henry said.

Ben stood guard with a shotgun while I went into the cell and put the manacles on Henry's wrists and ankles. He puffed on his cigar and hummed as I did.

Then we took him outside where Jim was waiting, also armed with a shotgun.

"Think you boys can handle me?" Henry asked, smiling.

There was a crowd of people present to witness the hanging. Henry walked through them as if he were taking a stroll, still puffing on his cigar. He looked at the scaffold and said, "That is good work. I had an uncle who was a carpenter. I used to help him some times and I know good work when I see it."

I took him up the steps and read the death warrant to the crowd. As I did, I saw Jess Griffin, grinning as if he were at a circus. I guess it was a circus to him.

I finished reading the warrant and turned to Henry to ask if there was any thing he wanted to say.

"No, I think that I have said enough for one life time," he replied.

He threw away the cigar and got on his knees to pray. I thought I was going to vomit as I watched him. Henry was smiling while he prayed.

Then he got up and raised his manacled hands in the air. "Goodbye all!" he cried.

The hang man put the black hood over his head. I felt my heart starting to beat faster and faster. I began to feel dizzy and had to hold on to a scaffold post.

"Draw it tighter," Henry told the hang man. I pressed my teeth together praying that I would not get sick in front of every body.

Then, just before the hang man sprang the trap, Henry cried

out again, this time in terror, his voice like that of a frightened boy.

"D——— you, Clay!" he cried. "*You didn't have to do it!*"

I felt as though all the blood in me was rushing out of my legs and into the scaffold as the trap door opened and Henry fell. I heard his neck crack and the sound was like a knife blade plunging straight into my heart.

My God! Henry! *I have killed you!*

Later: Every thing is finished now. I do not care.

I can not remember how I got down the scaffold steps after Henry was hanged. I think that Jim came up to help me but I am not sure. I know that he looked at me strangely. Later on, when I saw my face in a mirror, I knew why. I was as pale as a ghost.

Ben told me to come to his house but I pulled away from him. I walked over to Henry and put my hand on his chest. I could not believe that he was dead. I told Ben that I felt a heart beat and whispered to him that we had to get Henry to Doc Warner before it was too late.

He told me that I was imagining it because Henry was dead.

I turned away and walked to the first saloon I could find. I went inside and bought a bottle of rye and sat at a corner table to drink. I was cold and shaking and the first drink tasted like fire.

I intended to drink until I was unconscious. That was not to be. While I was sitting there, Jess Griffin and several of his friends came in. They stood at the counter and I heard them whispering. Griffin looked at me in the mirror and grinned.

It was all the push I needed. I got up and walked across the room where I started to bait him without mercy, wanting more than anything in the world to kill him. I called him a "mouth fighter" and a "yellow livered son of a b———."

He tried to back down with a joke because he was afraid. I would not let him. I insulted his father and mother and every person in his family. I told him that his mother and his sisters were all w———s. Still, he would not fight. I slapped his face and told him that I would murder him where he stood if he did not have the guts to defend himself.

He started to cry so I could not do it. I took what little pleasure there was in slapping him a few more times, then threw him out of the saloon and went back to my table.

About an hour later, when I went outside and started to cross the street, he tried to ride me down, shooting as he came. He almost knocked me over with his horse. I barely managed to avoid getting hit by leaping to the side and landing in the mud.

He wheeled his horse to gallop back and finish me. Pushing to my feet, I rested the barrel of my Colt across my left arm and, ignoring the hail of lead, brought him down with a single ball through the head.

Jim was the first to approach me after the shooting. He checked Griffin's body, then walked over to me.

"It is war to the knife now, Clay," he said.

"Good," I answered. *"Let it come."*

March 10, 1874

Ben came into the office.

"They are riding in," he said.

"How many?" I asked.

"I count eleven," he replied.

I nodded and looked toward Jim who was buckling on his gun belt. It was just past breakfast, maybe nine o'clock.

We did not exchange words as we armed ourselves. I had told them it was not their fight but they had paid no attention to me. It was their job to help keep the peace, they said. If the Griffins rode into Hays with iron on and my life as their intention, it was their duty to assist me. I should have argued but I could not. I needed them. Three of us together had some kind of chance. Alone, I was a dead man.

We finished getting ready and went outside onto the plank walk. It was a brisk morning with a little wind.

Roy Griffin and his three remaining sons plus his two brothers and five of his hands stopped in the street, looking toward Ben, Jim, and me.

The area was deserted, every one indoors. In the silence, there was a sound of footsteps on the walk and John appeared, carrying a sawed off shotgun. He took a position behind some crates in front of the mercantile store.

"Are you in on this?" Roy Griffin asked him.

"I am," John answered.

"Then get out from behind those crates and fight like a man," Griffin said.

"What is the matter? The odds not good enough for you now?" John asked in a mocking voice.

For a split second, Roy Griffin seemed to hesitate.

"Maybe you would rather back down," I told him.

He stiffened. "You murdered my boy," he said.

"He tried to ride me down and I shot him in self defense," I replied.

"Well, you will never shoot any one else," Griffin said.

For a moment, it seemed as though he was going to draw. Then he glanced at John and smiled. "We will be waiting for you at Kelly's Stable," he said. He pulled his horse around and they all rode down the street.

John came over to us.

"This is not your battle," I told him.

"I am a civilian," he said. "I can join if I want."

The four of us walked down the street to Kelly's Stable. Outside, dismounted, were the Griffins and their cow hands. The eleven of them stood in a line and we stopped to face them at a distance of approximately six yards.

"Surrender your weapons or face arrest," I told them.

"Die, you b——!" Griffin cried, clawing for his gun.

The next instant, the air exploded with a thunder of gun fire. The next, every one of us was obscured by a fog of powder smoke.

It was a scene from H———. The deafening roar of rifles, shotguns, and six-shooters. The fiery muzzle blasts lighting up twisted faces. The screams of wounded and dying men. The gushing sprays of blood. The bodies falling to the muddy ground.

I do not remember how I felt. I acted like a machine. I fired my shotgun, then dropped it, and drew a revolver. I emptied the revolver, drawing the second as I fired. I dropped the first and tossed the second into my right hand to continue firing without halt. I drew one of my Derringers as I fired. When the second Colt was empty, I dropped it and continued firing with the Derringer, drawing out the second Derringer as I did. I did not aim but fired quickly at the figures across from us. They kept falling. Lead whistled all around and the air was filled with the smell of burning powder.

It seemed to go on forever but, I am told, it lasted less than a minute. I lost all sense of what was real. A pistol ball knocked off my hat. Another grazed my right cheek. Several others tore at my clothes.

Otherwise, I was unhurt. John was shot dead beside me. Jim was hit in the chest and fell to the ground. Ben took lead in his shoulder and fell to one knee. Only I was standing, unharmed. As in a dream, I chased the three remaining Griffin cowhands down an alley, all of us reloading as we went.

I caught up with them behind the General Store and we exchanged fire. Not one of their shots came near me but I killed them all.

Then I heard footsteps running up behind me and I spun and fired without thought, killing Ben with a ball through his heart. He had been running to help me.

I could not comprehend what I had done. I knelt beside Ben and felt for his heart beat the way I did with Henry. I could not believe it was real. I was positive that I was going to wake up in my bed and find it all a dream.

I left Ben and went back to the stable yard. Townspeople were beginning to appear. They gaped at all the corpses. I helped Jim to his feet and led him to Doc Warner's office. He was bleeding badly.

When I came out of Doc Warner's, Streeter was there. His face was white. "You are no better than the Griffins," he said.

I walked past him. My legs felt like wood. I went to where John was lying dead, his body riddled with lead. His eyes were open and I closed them. I stood up. The street wavered around me. I thought I was going to faint. I walked down the alley. I was amazed to see that Ben was still there. I started to cry because I knew it was not a dream.

I picked up Ben and carried him to the undertaker's. I put him on a table and sat beside him, holding his hand and crying. I do not know how long I was there. Marion appeared and sat beside me. I felt as if the insides of my head were going to explode. She sat beside me, holding my hand and crying with me and I was the one who had killed her husband. Eleven men against us and he had survived only to be killed by me.

I am sitting in my room. I still feel dazed. My hands and feet are like wood. My head is numb. I still hope it is a dream. I know it is not.

John is dead because of me. I could have made him leave. I was selfish. I wanted him by my side because I needed him. Now he is dead.

Jim is badly hurt. Doc Warner says that he does not know if he will live.

Ben is dead. I killed him. Eleven men against us. Dozens of rifle and revolver balls fired at us yet he was only slightly hurt. And I killed him. *I killed him*. Without a thought. Spinning like a machine. Firing like a machine. Killing the best man I ever knew except for Mr. Courtwright. Ben Pickett was as true as steel and I killed him. In an instant. Ben is dead because of me. Because of *me*, not the Griffins. I can not believe it. It has to be a dream.

It was not a dream despite the fact that Clay rewrote that sentence sixteen times.

He had just taken part in the most real, *most bloody encounter ever to take place in the West which, later, became known as "Carnage At Kelly's Stable."*

This was the high water mark of Clay's career as a gunfighter. Never again was he to achieve such a summit of deadly efficiency with the six-shooter.

While making allowances for erratic observation, eye witness accounts indicate that, of the eleven men killed in the Griffin force, Clay killed a minimum of seven.

John Harris was killed almost immediately although it is logical to assume that, armed, as he was, with a shotgun, he took at least one of the Griffin men with him when he died.

By his own statement, Jim Clements killed two others, one of them Roy Griffin himself, before a severe chest wound knocked him to the ground.

Which leaves one life, accountable, no doubt, to Ben Pickett.

As Clay indicated in his journal, it must, indeed, have been a scene from H——, fifteen men exchanging shots as rapidly as possible, using shotguns, rifles, six-shooters and Derringers. At that close range, violent mortality must have come with extreme quickness. Estimates of the true length of the battle run as low as twenty-five seconds, which sounds perfectly feasible.

The incredible factor—here, we must openly admit, it seems more legendary than real—was that Clay did not receive a single wound more serious than a scratch across his right cheek. How this could have happened when, clearly, he would have been the principal target of the Griffin force, is difficult to understand.

Nonetheless, it did happen precisely in this manner. Perhaps it was because Clay knew instinctively which of his opponents was more likely to hit him and aimed for them first. Certainly, he was at the absolute zenith of his prowess in this battle, a veritable colossus of death, emptying and dropping one weapon after another, so rapidly that his fire never ceased for a fraction of a second until his ammunition was exhausted.

Whether the total fury of this encounter was what changed him will never be known. Surely, it had its affect on him. Whatever he had been involved in before, no battle could have matched, in brutal intensity, the Carnage at Kelly's Stable.

More than this, however, it was, doubtless, the loss of two of his closest friends that ultimately drove the spirit from him. Having just been the instrument of execution for Henry Blackstone, to now have been indirectly responsible for John Harris's death and directly responsible for Ben Pickett's must have

*been an emotional blow of severe force. Clay's entry, following
the battle, seems to have been made by a man almost literally
struck dumb by horrified disbelief.*

He was never the same again.

March 15, 1874

The Council called me in today.

They told me I was a murderer. A shame to my profession.
They said they were not going to renew my contract.

I did not say a word to them. While Mayor Gibbs was rant-
ing, I took off my badge and threw it on his desk. They do not
need me now because the Griffins are dead. The pawn has
done his job.

On my way back to the hotel, Bellingham approached me.
He did not know that the Council was not renewing my contract
or that I had quit. He told me that he had "searched his soul"
and decided that I represented "true law and order" in Hays and
had decided to "switch his hat" and come out in my favor.

If I could have laughed, I would have. After everything he
has written about me, to tell me that. I guess he needs another
"friend" now that the Griffins are dead.

I felt too tired to hit him so I just walked by him without a
word. The way I feel, I could not harm a man if he stood in
front of me with a gun in his hand and said that he was going
to kill me.

I am tired. I am going to rest. I will get out of Hays as soon
as I feel strong enough.

To H——— with this journal. To H——— with every
thing. I am going to finish this bottle of whiskey. Then I am
going to finish another bottle of whiskey. I am going to drink
until I pass out.

I have not told Marion. I am the only one who knows that I
killed him. I can not tell her. It would be too awful. I will
carry the secret to my grave.

* * *

I might add, at this point, that Mrs. Pickett died less than a year after her husband. Accordingly, as far as she is concerned, Clay has carried his secret to the grave.

Following the above, a month went by without another entry. What reports are available indicate that Clay sank into a state of almost total vegetation, sleeping and drinking and never leaving his room except to visit Marion Pickett and Jim Clements and bring fresh flowers to Ben Pickett's grave.

Clements started to recover from his wound in late April, and Clay decided to leave Hays and return to Hickman, hopefully to reconcile with Anne.

The day he left Hays, he lost his final friend.

April 29, 1874

I am sitting on the train as I write this. Hays is many miles behind me. I will never return to it. There is nothing there for me any more.

I was packing my bag when a man came running upstairs and knocked on my door. He told me that Jim had murdered his wife and a seventeen-year-old boy who worked in the General Store.

I rode out to Jim's house. There were some people standing in the street. One of them told me that I had better not go near the house or the "crazy man" inside would kill me.

I walked on to the porch and tried to open the door. It was locked.

"Get away from there," Jim said, inside.

"Jim, it is Clay," I told him.

He was silent for a while. Then he said, "You do not want to see this, Clay."

"Let me in," I replied.

He was silent again. Then I heard his footsteps and he unlocked the door. He was wearing his night shirt and an old robe. His hair was out of place. His eyes looked old.

"She is over there," he said, pointing.

I walked in to the parlor. There was a blood soaked blanket

over two bodies. I drew it back and saw Mary's white face staring up at me. Beside her was a young boy. Both of them were unclothed.

Jim came up beside me and looked down at his dead wife.

"She thought I was asleep upstairs," he said. "I found them in here. Mary screamed at me. She said that, since I could not 'service' her, she had a right to find some body else. My rifle was above the mantel. I took it down and shot them both."

He started to shiver and I put an arm around him.

"Listen," I said. "I understand. Get dressed, mount up and leave town."

"I have to be punished," he replied.

"You have been punished enough," I told him. "Get dressed and leave. Start over somewhere else."

He looked at me and, after a while, he smiled sadly and put his hand on my shoulder. "You have been a good friend, Clay," he said.

"Go up and dress," I said. "You can take my horse. It is already saddled. I will not need it anymore."

He nodded. "All right," he said.

I put the blanket over the bodies after he had left the parlor. I knew that I was helping him to break the law but I did not care. He was the only friend I had left. I was never going to tell him about Mary either.

The shot rang out as I was leaving the parlor. I ran upstairs.

Jim was lying on the bed, dead by his own hand. His Derringer had fallen to the floor. There was a hole in his chest and blood was running across his body.

I almost fell. My legs shook and I could not stop them. I sat on a chair and looked at Jim. After a long time, I got up and left the house. I returned to the hotel and finished packing. Then I went to the railroad station and sat there for two hours, waiting for the train to come.

I have been reading, in the *Gazette*, what really happened at Kelly's Stable. It is strange that I did not notice at the time.

It seems that a group of "hard working cow boys" riding into town for a little "well earned relaxation" were set upon by a "brutal police force in an unprovoked attack." Now the "head murderer" (me) is fleeing town and, under Sheriff Woodson's "upright aegis," law and order will, at long last, return to Hays.

Bellingham does not know it but he is beating a dead horse.

Some people nearby have recognized me. Word of my presence is moving through the car. I do not want to raise my head and see them staring at me. I will just keep writing.

Jim. Ben. John. Henry.

Me.

A week passed without an entry. Then, in Hickman . . .

May 6, 1874

I knew that I was fooling myself.

Anne is not interested in me any more. I think she was just hoping I had some money to give her.

She has received an offer of marriage from the man who owns the lumber yard in Hickman. She is going to accept, she said. She has already gone to a lawyer to get a divorce from me.

Melanie is better. She did not remember me.

Oh, why bother writing about it?

Why bother writing about anything?

Now Clay's last, close human contact had been severed and he was truly alone.

Again, a month passed without an entry. What Clay was doing during that time is any man's guess. In keeping with his past behavior, it is to be assumed that he spent the bulk of his time drinking, gambling, and consorting with the lower grade of female so common to the West.

Whatever he was doing, while he was doing it, the legend was increasing.

In contrast to the Hays Gazette, *the stories about Clay in the Eastern magazines and newspapers continued in an adulatory vein. (Sans my assistance, I am proud to state.)*

The headline for one of the stories recounting the now famous battle at Kelly's Stable reads: SINGLE-HANDED, KILLS SEVENTEEN MEN!

Despite the depths to which his will for life had fallen, his fame was at its peak.

It was a fame completely artificial now. No one in the East had any concept of him as a man. To them, he was untouchable. If there was blood in his veins, it was the blood of gods. Standing on the summit of some frontier Mount Olympus, he looked down, with august superiority, on lesser mortals.

No one realized that he had been thrust upon that mountaintop, condemned to stand alone.

So began the final phase of his life—wherein the legend ruled the man.

In dire need of funds, Clay agreed to appear in a play which was to have its "try out" in Albany, tour the state and surrounding areas, opening, at last, in New York City.

The play, Hero of The Plains, *was the epitome of all the ludicrous tales about him. Nonetheless, the offer from its producer was a handsome one and Clay accepted it rather than accept the various positions of City Marshal being submitted to him.*

June 18, 1874

I am sitting in my hotel room. I have just finished reading *Hero of The Plains*. It is as stupid as any story about me. It is worse.

When I picked up the manuscript at the theatre, the man who hired me shook my hand and said that this play is going to make me more famous than ever.

His name is Budrys and he has produced plays for some years, he told me.

I took the manuscript to my hotel room, took off my coat and boots, and stretched out on the bed to read it.

I was in a low state of mind, but, in spite of that, the play was so ridiculous it made me smile. I began to chuckle as I turned the pages, reading on. Finally, I had to laugh. There is nothing real in the play. I kill hundreds of Indians, and save wagon trains and towns, and shoot down dozens of outlaws and renegades.

Finally, I started laughing so hard, I could not read any more. I started writhing on the mattress, kicking my legs. Tears rolled down my cheeks. I dropped the manuscript on the floor. I was as hysterical as a woman. I pounded on the bed and howled with glee.

Then I realized that I had lost control. I was not laughing any more. I was crying and hitting the bed in fury. I was losing my mind, and I stopped myself.

For the first time in my life, I know what fear is.

Too bad Frank will never know it. But no one will read these words. It is the way I want it. I would not write them otherwise.

Rehearsals of Hero of The Plains *were degrading.*

Clay's entries make it clear how sickened by himself he was.

Standing on a Western street, facing an armed opponent, he had been the very image of steel-nerved deadliness.

Standing on a stage, attempting to mouth the pompous dialogue of the play, he was absurd.

Embarrassed by the words and how he spoke them as well as by the staring actors, he stumbled and stammered. His movements were clumsy and inept. The director, in an agony of prescience, foresaw complete disaster and did not care who knew about it.

Clay foresaw it too but had to continue. A contract had been signed and money paid and he was still a man who honored his obligations.

What neither of them realized was that people would be attending the play for one thing only and that was to see the man who was a myth—the legendary Clay Halser. Whether he was actually portraying himself in a "True Account Of His Death-Defying Adventures" was beside the point. That he moved and spoke with awkward blundering was not important.

That it was him—*Clay Halser, in the flesh—was all that mattered.*

July 23, 1874

"First Night" as they say!

Sitting in my room. Drunk as a hoot owl. Don't give God d———— about it!

Could not face the audience sober. Drank all day. Came to the theatre half booze blind. They did not know. I can hold it. Stand up. My breath maybe. Who cares? To H———— with them!

Could not remember lines. Kept missing them. Every body laughed. Did not care. To H———— with every body! Whole play falling apart.

Saloon Scene. Supposed to tell my "comrades" about an adventure. Shot down twenty-seven outlaws "six guns spewing leaden death!" *That* again! S———!

Bar tender in play hands me a drink. Thought it *was* a drink. Every one on stage cried, *"Tell us the story, Marshal Halser!"*

Took a swallow of the drink. Spat it all over the stage, on half the actors.

"Who the H———— put cold tea in a whiskey bottle?" I roared.

Audience loved it. Roared back with laughter. Made me grin. Forgot the God d————d play! Said, "I don't tell stories 'til I get some *real* whiskey!"

Thought I was fooling. Was not. Bar tender poured another glass of tea. I poured it on his head. Audience roared. *"Real* whiskey!" I cried. Audience loved it. "Get him whiskey!" they shouted. They began to chant. "Whiskey, whiskey, whiskey!" as I pounded on the bar.

Some one brought a bottle of rye. Audience cheered. I grabbed the bottle and pulled out the cork with my teeth. Spat out the cork. Audience loved it. Laughed and clapped. Took a swig of the whiskey. *Real stuff*. I made believe it was *hot*.

Stamped my foot and howled like a coyote. Audience loved it. Laughed loud. Applauded. Hit of the evening!

I forgot the play. Who needs the play? Dumb thing. Started to tell about Henry and Bill Bonney and us in the trench house. I understand though. Not tell the truth. That is not what they want. They want lies. Made it *two hundred* Indians! Made us only five men! Killed the last fifty Indians with knives and hatchets! Blood up to our knees!

I expected laughter. Gales of laughter. No. They cheered! J——— C———. They cheered! Stood on their feet, applauding. "Standing ovation," they call it. Cheering! *Bravo! Bravo!*

Stared at them like a dumb man. Can not understand. I lied to them! Stupid, dumb, crazy lies! And they believed every G——— d———d word!

To H——— with people!

Whether Clay ever truly understood that the legend had enveloped him is hard to ascertain.

His confusion in this entry seems complete. True, he was drunk when he wrote it, but it is my conviction that he never was truly aware of how he had been victimized by the myth— no, not even to the end. Being a man with a straightforward, logical turn of mind, he seemed, always to attempt to locate some connection between himself and the legend which surrounded him.

He never seemed to comprehend the obvious fact that there was no such connection; that Clay Halser, the man, and Clay Halser, the legend, were two entirely separate entities.

This is, in essence (perhaps), the gist of the phenomenon which destroyed him.

Having succeeded in captivating an audience without adhering to the manuscript of Hero of The Plains, *Clay continued doing so, achieving a kind of freewheeling (and half-drunken) style somewhere in between the play and his own heavy-handed sense of drama—and humor.*

Accordingly, the play became workable and the company began to tour New York and its adjacent states.

Off stage, Clay continued to be a "loner," unable to make friends with anyone in the company. In general, they either regarded him with fearful awe or, in the majority of cases, with superior contempt, believing him to be a poseur and a fraud, a belief no doubt justified in light of his behavior on stage which, of course, was all they knew of him.

Occasionally, he spent some time with various of the actresses in the company but received no comfort from them and no sense of communication.

In addition, the preponderance of "deviates" among the male actors put him off completely and he was compelled, on several occasions, to let it be known that any such approaches toward him would be met with violent hostility.

As a result of all this, he was pretty much left to himself by the other members of the cast and his days and nights were lonely ones, the long, empty hours made palatable by heavy drinking.

The first result of this intemperance occurred in early September.

September 10, 1874

I am locked in my room. I am afraid to go out. I am afraid to drink and I am afraid to not drink. I am shaking so bad that I can hardly write.

There is the scene in Act Two. A "shootout" between "Black Bart" and me. I always win.

Tonight, I heard him walking up behind me on the street set and I turned.

It was Ben.

I stared at him in horror. "Ben?" I said.

He looked at me. His face was white and streaked with mud and there was blood flowing from his chest.

I screamed and ran from the stage and theatre. I ran all the way to the hotel and to my room. I am sitting here now. I have put a chair against the door and it is locked.

But locked doors can not keep away the dead.

It was the whiskey. I know it was the whiskey. I must not drink so much. I swear I will stop before it is too late.

Ben. Oh, God. Ben looking at me with those sweet, grave eyes. The man I loved and killed. Ben.

Oh, God! I *saw* him!

Firmly believing that whiskey alone caused him to suffer his hallucination, Clay attempted to cut down on his consumption.

An added impetus to this resolve was the fact that the tour was soon to take him near Pine Grove. Despite apprehensions, he hoped that a visit to his hometown would provide him with a needed boost.

It did exactly the reverse.

To his utter disheartenment, he discovered that he had even lost his identity with his own family who, in spite of knowing him all his life, tended to regard him as the super man of violence portrayed in all the articles and stories and not as the young man they remembered.

Mary Jane Silo (Mary Jane Meecham for many years by then) was remote and uncomfortable in his presence. Whatever relationship they had had was entirely a thing of the past and, it seemed to Clay, that past was irrevocably dead.

Indeed, it was as if Clay Halser, the man, was also dead while pretending to be him was this frightening impostor who looked and sounded like him but was, quite obviously, without his soul.

It was in Pine Grove that Clay suffered his second hallucination, one far more terrifying than the first.

October 23, 1874

I have to stop drinking or I am going to lose my mind I *know* it.

It is four o'clock in the morning. I am still cold from what happened.

I was supposed to be in Fort Wayne last night. The "Hero

of The Plains" was not there, however. He was here in Pine Grove, drinking.

I should never have come here. I was a fool to think that it would work out. No one knows me for what I am. They have all read the stories and I am unreal to them. Even my Mother does not know me! It was like being with a stranger. My brothers. My sisters. All strangers to me. I thought that Ralph, at least, would see me as I am. All he did was ask about Indians and how many I had killed bare handed. I could not get away from the house fast enough.

I went to *The Green Horse*. It looked different to me. Smaller, more dingy. I sat at the same table where I had played cards with Menlo. I sat in the chair that I had used. It gave me a strange feeling. Did it all start that night? Was it the beginning?

Some local men came in and gathered around. I tried to be friendly with them but they held back. I was desperate to get a laugh out of them. I thought if I could make myself foolish in their eyes, they would know that I was really just a man after all.

I told them the wildest story I could make up. I told them that I held back a lynch mob of three hundred and fifty people armed only with a rusty, unloaded revolver. I waited for their laughter but it did not come. They wanted to hear the rest of the story! I lost my temper and told them to get away from me.

They scattered like sheep. They were afraid of me. They hated me too. I saw the way they whispered about me. Men always hate what they fear.

I drank by myself. I sat there drinking rye and trying to think what I should do. I could not make up my mind. I do not like it here in the East but I do not want to go back West either. At least men do not challenge me here. There are no boys with pimples on their faces traveling distances to "try" me.

I do not know how long I drank before my brain got muddled. I thought I would rest and I laid my head on my arms on the table. It was late. There was only one other man in the saloon beside myself and that was the bar tender. I guess he wanted to close the saloon but did not dare to tell me to leave.

It is all so clear. I do not see how it could have been unreal. It was so *clear*.

I heard a voice say, "Howdy, Clay."

I lifted my head from the table and looked around. The room seemed to ripple like colorless jelly.

I saw Henry standing in the doorway.

My God, I swear that he was real! I stared at him, a hundred thoughts tumbling through my head. Ben had been wrong! I *had* felt a heartbeat and someone had rescued Henry and saved his life. It was *him*. He had followed me back East.

Then he moved outside and I jumped to my feet. I was dizzy and almost fell. I staggered to the door, calling out his name. The bar tender looked at me but did not say a word.

I pushed through the bat wing doors. "Henry!" I cried. I looked around the dark street but I could not see him?

Fear chilled me. Was he hiding in the shadows, waiting to kill me for what I had done to him?

I threw myself to the ground and looked around. The street ran like water before my eyes. "All right, go ahead!" I told him. "Shoot!"

There was no shot. I looked around. "Henry!" I shouted.

"Here!" he said.

I saw him down the street, standing near a store front.

I pushed to my feet and ran after him. I did not care if he was there to kill me. I deserved to be killed.

When I reached the place he had been standing, he was gone.

I looked around. "Henry, don't hide!" I told him. "If you want to kill me, *do* it! Just let me see your face!"

"Here I am!" he said.

I whirled and saw him standing in an alley. I ran after him. He turned and went away. I ran around a corner. He was standing twenty feet away from me, near a hitching post.

"All right, if you won't draw, I will!" I cried. I snatched out my revolver and fired.

Henry ducked away. I ran to where he had been standing. "Don't do this to me, Henry!" I shouted. "Face me like a man!"

"Clay!" he cried.

He was standing down the street.

I ran after him but he was gone. He was across the street from me. I chased him there and he went into another alley. I cursed and fired at him until my gun was empty. Lights went on in windows. People looked out at me.

I chased him all the way to the graveyard. He stood on a grave and laughed at me. "You will never catch me, old fellow!" he said.

Then he vanished and I fell on the ground, crying. "Henry, please come back," I begged. "Let me see your face."

He can not come back. He is dead. He was not in the doorway or the street or in the alleys. I know that now. He was a vision in my mind. The whiskey again.

Yet it was so clear! I remember what my Gran said when I was a boy. "The dead do walk at times," she said. "When they have need."

Sweet God, *do* the dead walk?

If so—*how many will walk with me?*

After that night, Clay was never to see his hometown again. Returning to the company, he continued touring with Hero of The Plains.

Approximately one month later, the play opened in New York City.

It was a huge success, not only the "masses" turning out in force but all of "high society" as well.

Clay, just drunk enough not to give a d——— (although, because of fear, he had tapered off his alcoholic consumption), performed with bombastic theatricality and the cheering and applause—albeit partially satirical, I feel—was deafening.

At the time, I was in Kentucky and unable to attend. To this day, I am not sure if I regret it or am grateful. Although it would have been good to see Clay again, I think it would have saddened me to see him making sport of himself.

That night, following the show, he was taken to dinner by Miles Radaker. On this occasion, Clay revealed that underneath the veneer of foolishness he had assumed, there still remained part of a man of ice-grained substance.

November 27, 1874

Went out tonight with Miles Radaker, the man who wrote that first article about me more than three years ago.

I gather he has made a tidy fortune exploiting what he called "The Halser Chronicle." In gratitude, he and his current mistress (he told me that when she had left the table) took me out to dinner.

I should not have gone. It is the first time in my life that I have been in such a "posh" restaurant. I made a fool of myself, not knowing which piece of silver to use, not knowing how to eat with delicacy, and not knowing how to conduct the "chit chat of the elite" as Radaker called it.

His mistress—Claudine—is a beautiful young woman. I think she liked me or was attracted to me any way. Or to the legend, I do not know. What I do know is that it became clear very soon that they were having fun at my expense, pretending to be interested in what I had to say but snickering in such a manner that I knew they took me for a perfect fool. I believe that Radaker truly thought me a country bumpkin who believed all the stories.

I held my temper as long as I could. When they started to make remarks about my clothes and hair, though, I decided to turn the table. I took my Derringer out of my inside coat pocket and laid it on the table between Radaker and myself.

"Here is a game we used to play," I told him. I cocked the Derringer and drew back my hand. "We put our hands on our laps and count to three. The one who grabs the Derringer first gets to live."

Radaker smiled. He seemed amused. "What are you talking about?" he asked.

"A game," I said. I put my hands on my lap. "Put your hands on your lap," I told him. "I will count to three."

"What are you talking about?" he asked. There was a quaver in his voice.

"One," I said.

"Wait a second," he told me. I saw a dew of sweat breaking out on his forehead. "What is this, a joke?" he asked.

"No," I said. "It is a game we played to discover which of us was the real fighter and which could only fight with his mouth."

"All right, all right," Radaker laughed nervously. "Very funny, Mr. Halser. Now put that thing away before it goes off."

"It *will* go off," I said. "In the hand of the first of us to grab it."

"This is not amusing to me any more," he said. There was quite a bit of sweat on his forehead by then.

"It is not supposed to be amusing," I said. "It is a game of life and death. Put your hands on your lap."

"I will do no such thing," he said. His voice shook badly.

"Then I will have to do it by myself," I said. "One."

"Stop this," Radaker said.

"Two," I said.

"For God's sake, are you *mad?*" he asked.

"You had better get ready to grab for it," I said. "Or you are going to die."

"What are you *talking* about?" he asked.

"You are very good with your mouth," I said. "Let us see how good you are with your hand."

"All right, I apologize," he said. "You are very clever."

"One," I said.

"Stop it, stop it," he said. He was sweating hard now and his face was white.

"I will start the count again," I said.

"For God's sake," Radaker began.

"One," I said.

"Halser, if it's money . . ."

"Two," I said.

He pushed back from the table with a whimper.

"Three!" I said. I snatched up the Derringer so fast that he could not even blink before I had it in my hand. I pulled the trigger and the hammer clicked against the empty chamber. Radaker lurched back in his chair and fell to the floor with a cry.

I put the Derringer in my pocket and stood up.

"Good night, Mr. Radaker," I said. "I have enjoyed the dinner. Thank you very much."

I left the restaurant. It was the first time I have felt any pleasure in a long time.

The pleasure is gone now. I am tired of the people back here. I may go back out West after all. Despite the perils, it is, at least, a place where I can breathe my own kind of air.

Four days later, following a night's heavy drinking, Clay's "career" as a stage actor terminated abruptly.

December 1, 1874

I am leaving the show. Tomorrow morning, I am going to catch an early train and start back West.

We had a matinee performance today. There were a lot of children present. I had a headache from the drinking I did last night.

In between each scene, I told the stage manager to tell the spotlight man not to shine it in my eyes because it made my headache worse. He never did it and I got angrier by the minute.

During the first act intermission, I got my Derringer from my dressing room and loaded it.

When the next act started and the spotlight hit my eyes again, I pulled out the Derringer and shot it out.

Then something took me by the hand and walked me to the footlights. I looked out over all the faces in the audience. I saw the children looking at me, and suddenly I could not bear the idea that they thought they were seeing truth on that stage.

I do not remember exactly what I said to them but it was something like this.

"You have been watching nonsense, do you know that? Not a word spoken up here has been a truthful one.

"You have come to see me, Clay Halser, the Great Western Hero.

"Do you want to know what it was really like out there? The truth and not the nonsense you have all been looking at?

"I will tell you.

"There was nothing pretty about it. There was nothing brave and gallant.

"I had a wife and a child but my wife left me because she could not stand facing each day, wondering if I would be coming back for supper on my own two feet or stretched out dead on a board. I was not a *Hero of The Plains* to her.

"I had five good friends but now they all are dead. They did not die like characters in this play. The blood they spilled was real.

"I had a friend named Mr. Courtwright you probably have read about. He was murdered by three hired renegades. I followed those men and when I found them, I did not say, 'Draw, you varmint,' or anything like that. I did not behave like the *Hero of The Plains*. I walked over to the table they were sitting at and shot them down in cold blood because they had murdered my friend.

"I had a friend named John Harris. You probably have read about him. He was a good, honest man. He was shot down by my side and died without a word. There was nothing 'thrilling' about his death. He was just filled with lead. He was not a *Hero of The Plains*.

"I had a friend named Jim Clements. He was brave and honest. He was wounded helping me at Kelly's Stable. He married a woman who had almost been murdered in a w——— house where she worked. While she was recovering, Jim fell in love with her.

"I never told him she had been a prostitute. But, while he was recovering from his wounds, she began consorting with a seventeen-year-old boy. Jim found them together in the parlor and he shot them both dead with his rifle. Then he went upstairs and killed himself with a Derringer."

There was a murmur of shocked voices by then. I saw mothers and fathers rushing their children up the aisles but I kept on.

"I had a friend named Ben Pickett. You probably have read about him. He was a good, brave man and the best Deputy a City Marshal ever had. Do you know how he died? Not at the hands of the Griffins at all. No. *I* shot him. *Me.* I was so worked up by the fight at Kelly's Stable that, when he ran up behind me to help me, I spun around without thinking and shot him dead. I killed my own friend. I was not much of a hero when I did that.

"I had a friend named Henry Blackstone. You probably have read about him. He was a strange, young fellow but a friend of mine. I sold him for money. He could have escaped but I would not let him. I wanted the thousand dollars reward money offered for him. He could have killed me and escaped but he didn't want to hurt me. So they hanged him. He was my friend and I was the one who put the noose around his neck. Do you know what a neck sounds like when it breaks? Like a piece of wood being snapped in two. I did that to my friend, Henry. Then I goaded Jess Griffin into a fight even though he was afraid of me. I did it even though I knew his family would have to seek revenge after I had killed him. And they did and John Harris and Ben Pickett were killed. Because of me.

"That is just a small part of what it was like in the West. I know it is not as exciting as *Hero of The Plains* but that is the way it was and I can not change the facts."

There were a few people who applauded when I left the stage but mostly there was bedlam. People do not like a legend to have flesh and blood.

Budrys said that, if I leave, he will get even with me, somehow. I told him to go to H————.

Later: Budrys really meant what he said, the son of a b————.

I have just finished washing off the blood and am sitting in my room, a power of cuts and bruises.

I feel great!

I was down in the hotel saloon, having a drink, when these three big galoots came in. I was standing at the corner and they stood beside me, two on one side, one on the other. We were the only customers.

"Howdy, Buffalo Bill," the one on my left said.

I did not look at him.

"I said *howdy*, Buffalo Bill," he repeated.

I looked at him.

"Are you talking to me?" I asked.

"I ain't talking to your brother," he said.

"I did not think you were," I replied, "since my brother is not Buffalo Bill, either."

"You *are* Buffalo Bill," he said.

"You are wrong," I told him.

"And you are a dirty, stinking liar who eats s———," he came back. "What do you think of that?"

That was when I realized that Budrys had hired them to take his anger out of my skin.

"Permit me," I said. I finished my drink and put down the glass. I sighed with contentment. Then I knocked that big, ugly b——— halfway across the room with a blow to the jaw that had my fullest cooperation.

The other two lunged at me. I gave one the whiskey bottle right across the face. The other one, I gave a knee in the b———s and a fist in the eye.

By then the first man was back at me and the "battle was joined" as the *Hero of The Plains* used to tell his "comrades."

I do not say it was an easy fight. Those fellows were strong enough and they did put their heart and soul to it. But they were dudes. I mean, a man who has not learned to fight "western style" has not learned to fight.

I used every trick I knew (all dirty) and gave it to them knuckle and skull. By the time I had done with them, those three, poor fellows were stretched out cold and bloody on the floor.

I poured myself a drink and threw it down. It tasted like the nectar of the gods. It was good to win a fight again. I have lost so many in the past year.

"Send the repair bill to Mr. Budrys at the Lyceum Theatre," I told the bar keep. "He will be glad to pay for all damages."

I gave him a smile and left.

Lord, one of my teeth just fell out!

No entries of interest occur for more than a month and a half following the above.

Clay returned to the frontier and began to follow old paths, gambling, drinking, and spending occasional time with the lesser females of the towns he frequented.

As further indication that the legend had, by then, so surpassed the man as to make him literally unrecognizable, the following entry is displayed. Clay was, at the time, in Dawes in the Indian Nations.

January 25, 1875

I was sitting in a saloon this morning when it happened. I was reading the local newspaper. The story of prime interest to me was headlined CLAY HALSER IN TOWN! It told how the "nationally, nay, internationally" famous Marshal-Gun Fighter is "passing through" on his way to "who knows what incredible adventures." I know what. *None.*

Any way, I was reading when there was a sound of gunfire next door. I mean *lots* of gunfire.

I did not intend to find out what had caused it. How ever, a cry went up which, I admit, somewhat stirred my curiosity.

"Clay Halser has been killed!" was the cry.

Every one ran out of the saloon. I got up to follow.

"My God, to view those storied remains," an old man said as I went outside.

"It will be a thrill," I said.

He and I walked to the next door saloon and pushed in through the bat wing doors. There was quite a crowd.

I was lying on the floor, dead.

As a matter of truthful fact, the man did somewhat resemble me. He was dressed in gambler's black and was about the same height and build. There were two pearl-handled revolvers clutched in his hands however. A little too fancy for me.

It must have been one H——— of a shootout. There were an awful lot of holes in that man. I counted five, at first. Blood and people hid the rest from view.

One of the customers was telling how it happened.

"Just came in, mean drunk," he said. "Picked a fight with Bobby there and, by God, Bobby won."

I looked at Bobby. He must have been all of eighteen years of age. He looked like a kid at Christmas, flushed and over joyed.

I moved closer to take a good look at myself. There were seven bullet holes in me. Bobby had taken no chances.

"Should have thought that one would be enough," I said.

The old man was standing next to me. "Against *Halser*?" he demanded. "Are you *insane*?"

I did not argue the point. I left the saloon and went back to the hotel. I think I had better move on. Sooner or later, someone will discover that that body is not quite me. Then Bobby will feel obliged to find the real me and repeat his triumph. Except that he will end up in a pine box. And I am in no mood to start killing again.

I wonder if it would be a good idea to change my name and appearance. I could grow a mustache like Ben's and call myself . . .

Blackstone! that is what I will do.

Henry will live again.

Despite his resolve—which seems to have been a wise one— Clay did not change his name. He grew the mustache but went no further than this in the attempt to prevent others from recognizing him.

Whether this was a result of apathy or ego it is hard to determine. He might have decided not to bother. He might have

*tried, then given it up. When one spends his lifetime writing
and speaking his true name, it is difficult to remember to write
and speak a false one however strong the intention to do so.*

*On the other hand, it may have been ego; a reluctance to
remove himself entirely from the myth. It is possible that man
and legend had become so inextricably bound by then that he
was unable to separate them anymore.*

*An uneventful month passed by, Clay continuing his life
as a gambler. While never a truly accomplished card player,
he was good enough to win if his opponents were not of the
highest caliber. Remembering past experiences, he saw to it
that he never played with members of the professional "circuit." Accordingly, his winnings always exceeded his losses
by enough of a margin to support him.*

*The next noteworthy entry occurred when Clay was in
Topeka, Kansas.*

February 28, 1875

Maybe I can get by with my "gift of gab" as they say. After
accusing others of being "mouth fighters" all these years, it
turns out I am not too bad a one myself.

I was having a game of Faro in the *Cimarron Saloon* this
afternoon when a gaunt, whey-faced gent came walking to
the table on legs as stiff as logs. Oh, God, here it comes, I
thought.

"Halser?" he said.

I looked up at him. His face was so white, it could have
been dipped in biscuit batter. His hands were shaking. Still, I
knew that he had "made up his mind" to face me.

"Before you say another word," I told him, "let me tell you
what will happen to you if you do not turn around and walk
away from here. First of all, you can not win. You are shaking
like a wheat stalk in a wind storm. You will probably drop
your gun, assuming you get it out of your scabbard at all.

"On the other hand, I have been a gunfighter for ten years
now. (We mouth fighters like to stretch the facts.) I am so fast

that you will have three bullets in your body before you can fire one. They will hurt like H————. I can not promise you a quick death either. You might drag on two or three days in utter agony before you die. Is is worth it? You do not look as though you want to die. So just turn around and leave. I will not hold it against you. I will admire you for your ripe good sense."

That poor fellow turned and moved out of the *Cimarron* like a sleepwalker. After he had left, a great laugh went up from all. "Shall we continue with our game now?" I said.

Those idiots applauded me! For a moment, I thought I was back on the d———— stage, doing *Hero of The Plains*.

Later: I am in a strange mood. Part of me is happy and part of me is afraid. The two feelings are mixed and I can not seem to separate them.

Maybe if I write down how they came about, it will grow clear to me why I can not get them apart in my mind.

I went to the theatre after supper tonight. They were performing a comedy called "The Dude Finds Out."

I bought myself a box near the stage because I felt like sitting alone. I brought a bottle of rye with me and had a drink or two as the play went on.

I had not bothered looking at the program so the first I knew of it was in the second act when a character entered who was referred to as "bawdy Aunt Alice."

To my surprise and pleasure it turned out to be Hazel Thatcher.

I was close to the stage (being in the box) but, when she saw me the first time, I do not think she recognized me, probably because of the mustache. Then, during a scene in which she had to listen to a long speech by "Ned the Dude," she peered at me in curiosity. I raised my hand and smiled at her. "Clay," I said with my lips.

She looked delighted and the next few lines she had came out badly.

I confess to being so absorbed in the welcome sight of her that I never noticed what was going on. If I had been a quarter so careless in Caldwell or Hays, they would have buried me ten times over.

The first I knew of it was Hazel looking across my shoulder in dread and breaking the scene by shouting, "Look *out* Clay!"

Before her words were out, I threw myself to the right grabbing at my revolver. A shot rang out close by, almost deafening me. Rolling over as fast as I could, I shot up at the figure in the shadows. He screamed and doubled over dropping his gun.

I stood and put my Colt away, moving to the man who was sitting on the floor of the box, hands pressed across his bleeding stomach, groaning with pain. It was the fellow I had talked out of fighting me this afternoon! I guess the laughter which greeted his departure had been more than he could stand.

Two men came and carried him away, and I said, "Please continue," to the cast and bowed to them. There was applause and the play went on.

I was not as blithe as I sounded. My hands were shaking and there was a cold knot in my stomach I could not untie. Later, I had to step out to relieve my b———s.

I am glad that I survived, of course. I am grateful to Hazel for having saved my life.

But I am shaken that I would have been killed if it had not been for her. I am shaken that I shot the man where I did. In the past, my shots, however rushed, almost never failed to kill men instantly, most often through the heart.

The man will die, of course. He will die exactly as I told him he would—in two or three days, in utter agony. But I told him that to frighten him. I did not really believe it.

Now it is *so*. And I am shaken. Have I lost my skill? How is it possible that he was able to sneak up behind me like that without me hearing a sound? Is it the whiskey again?

I am afraid, but I do not know how to deal with the fear. I feel anxious, and my heart is beating strangely, and my breath is hard to control.

What a thing to happen just as I find Hazel again. For that is what is making me happy. I am going to pick her up after she has changed her clothes. We will have a late supper and, I hope, spend the night together. Maybe I will sleep without the dreams tonight. *(The first reference Clay ever makes to (doubtless bad) dreams. F.L.)*

After the show, I went backstage and we held on to each other for a long time, kissing as though we were hungry for each other. "To have you back," she murmured. "To have you back."

I might have spoken the same words. To have her back. Someone to be with. Someone I know. It makes me very happy.

If only I was not afraid as well.

To rediscover Hazel Thatcher at this point in his life was clearly a moving experience to Clay. So moving, in fact, that his eyes and ears endowed Hazel with a charm she no longer possessed—if, indeed, she had ever possessed it at all.

Time had not been kind to her. The desolate life she had led made her look far older than her thirty-nine years.

Clay never knew it but, some months prior to this meeting, I had run across her in Wichita.

She had come up to my hotel room and tried to get some money from me, telling me that she was Clay's "old friend" and that she had heard "so much about me" from Clay and wished that she knew me better "because I was his friend." Could I loan her ten dollars for a few days? The poor woman even offered, obliquely, to sell her "favors" to me for the amount.

I wish I could describe the sense of utter corruption she conveyed to me. She may have been a "handsome" woman at one time; Clay seems to have thought so, at any rate. But that night, every second of her dissipated life showed in her pale, somewhat bloated face, especially in her green eyes and in the downward cast of her over-painted mouth.

That Clay was moved to see her again can only demonstrate the measure of his loneliness.

She was more than just a woman to him then. His entries make this clear. She represented, to him, the happy past which he longed to recapture.

As for her, Hazel Thatcher was, doubtless, fully as delighted to see him. Her path had been a downward one since they had last met. Carl was dead, a victim of alcohol poisoning. She drank heavily herself. No longer able to attract men of any taste whatever, she had been forced to be content, for the indulgence of her physical desires, with men of less and less degree, stable hands and the like.

To have Clay reappear so unexpectedly must have been, to her, like Manna from Heaven. Consequently she, no doubt, displayed every last iota of allurement she could manage, not realizing that it was not necessary; that Clay, alone and dispirited, would not have left her for anything.

So, each of them needing the other desperately—neither seeing the other with an eye the least bit objective—they fell into groping resumption of their old affair. Shortly after, Clay became convinced that, this time, it was genuine love and, when Hazel mentioned marriage, he could not resist.

Disenchantment set in quickly.

March 17, 1875

I never knew Hazel had such a sharp tongue. I never saw evidence of it before.

March 21, 1875

Another fight today. Hazel thinks I should take a job as City Marshal somewhere. I told her no.

April 3, 1875

How could I have thought she was beautiful?

Now I know why she prefers to ———— in the dark.

April 9, 1875

I am beginning to think that Hazel is stupid.

April 28, 1875

Hazel said I look like an old man. She said she should have married the stories instead of me.

May 5, 1875

Another battle. She insists I take a peace officer job. I told her that it will be snowing in H——— before I do that.

I am making enough on my gambling to keep going. Of course, when the acting company leaves, Hazel will be without a job.

Unless she goes with them.

May 17, 1875

I am so tired of squabbling with her. I cannot sleep late anymore. She wakes me up each morning with a new complaint. She wants to have children and a home now!

A H——— of a Mother she would make!

May 25, 1875

"Get a job as a peace officer in a *peaceful* town then!" she yelled.

"You stupid b———!" I told her. "Any town that is peaceful does not *need* a peace officer!"

* * *

I thought it was going to be so nice with Hazel. It is a nightmare.

June 3, 1875

She wants me to go back on the stage!

"Cash in on yourself, for C———'s sake!" she said.

She has some bright idea about us getting people to give us money so we can start a publishing house. Then *I* will write stories *about myself* and "we will be rich!"

She is such a stupid woman.

June 17, 1875

She called me a "three-toed b———" and I hit her.

June 23, 1875

I told her I might do some mining.

"And in the meantime, what?" she said. "Sleep late every morning? Spend your afternoons and nights gambling while I work?"

She says she is going to quit her job with the play. Let her. There are always w——— houses.

July 4, 1875

Independence Day.

I wish I was independent of Hazel.

July 12, 1875

She read my journal today and laughed at me. I hit her and she scratched my neck until the blood ran.

Then she cried and begged me to take a job as City Marshal. She said that she is getting old and wants a family of her own. She pleaded with me to help her. When I said I would not, she scratched my neck again.

July 19, 1875

I am thinking of leaving Hazel and doing some mining. A man can make a fortune in the gold or silver lodes.

I can not bear to touch her. She does not wash.

July 30, 1875

I am drunk. I am sick of Hazel. I wish I had not married her. We fight all the time. She curses and throws things at me. She hates me because I will not "be a man" and take a City Marshal job somewhere and let her have a home and family.

I do not hate her. I feel sorry for her. I feel sorry for myself. There is nothing in the past. The past is dead. John and Ben are lucky. Jim and Henry are lucky. Mr. Courtwright is lucky. They died in their time.

I have gone beyond mine. I am useless.

What would it have been like to marry Mary Jane and be a farmer in Pine Grove?

So it went from day to day. The marriage was doomed and both of them knew it. Still, they attempted to keep it alive.

With Clay, it was—his entries make apparent—mostly from

a sense of loyalty because Hazel had saved his life and was a meaningful part of it.

With Hazel it was—I feel certain—pure and simple desperation. She recognized that, despite their differences, Clay was still her only chance. If they separated, she would go, forthwith, to the bottom, ending up in some trail town brothel. (A fate she has, I fear, suffered by this time.)

The weeks and months dragged by, Clay sleeping until afternoons, then gambling and drinking until the early morning hours; Hazel working in the theatre, then, when the theatre company left Topeka, taking a job as a saloon "girl."

Their life together was increasingly empty and dissatisfying. Both of them drank to excess, their conflicts taking on the aspect of drunken brawls replete with mutual physical violence, the details of which I will not exhibit.

Clay began suffering regularly from nightmares, often waking up, screaming. Several times he experienced further hallucinations, on one occasion becoming so convinced that Henry Blackstone's vengeance-seeking corpse was waiting for him in their hotel room that he would not return there for two days.

Money became a larger problem all the time, Clay's win-loss balance shifting to the debit side more often than not. He sold his horse and saddle, his shotgun, his second Colt, finally his Derringers, keeping one revolver for self-defense which, fortunately, he was not called upon to use during this period. If he had been, it is doubtful whether he would have survived because of his inordinate drinking.

Withal, restless, discontented and unhappy, he continued to maintain his marriage to Hazel, wondering, almost longingly, when it was going to end.

The one interesting entry during this time has to do with his meeting of a man who was his equal in fame if not in skill.

September 23, 1875

I was sitting in the *Colorado House* playing poker when a cheer went up behind me and I looked around.

A tall man dressed in black had entered the saloon. His hair was long and light-colored and his mustache drooping. It was Hickok.

I returned to my game but knew, from that instant on, that some one would bring us together, hopefully toward some violent incident. I made up my mind that—as in Morgan City—I would defer to him in all things. I was not afraid of him. I still am not. I simply did not care to face anyone in a life and death contest. I hope I never have to face a man in that fashion again.

My apprehension proved groundless. Hickok had no more desire to clash heads with me than I had to do the same with him. We were brought together (as I knew we would be) and sat with each other, drinking and chatting. I suppose it was a thrill for all those in the saloon to see two "legends" sitting in the corner.

Hickok is no more a legend than I am. In truth, he has gone through much of what I have. I feel that he has managed to live with it better than I have but his existence has been no bed of roses, either.

The first thing I asked him after we were together was whether he remembered hurrahing me in Morgan City.

He smiled a little. "No, sir, I do not," he said. "However, I dare say that you understand, now, why I acted as I did."

"I do," I said. "Being a cow town Marshal is not the most relaxing job in the world."

He chuckled at that. "No, it is not," he agreed.

It was a pleasant evening, I must say. I think that he enjoyed it too. Who, more than me, could understand what he has experienced—just as who, more than he, could appreciate what I have been through? I will not say that we "poured out" our hearts exactly. Neither of us are the kind to do so.

Still, we did chat, at length, about our experiences. It is interesting to note the similarities.

Both of us were born in the Middle West and grew up in like ways.

Both of us fought in the War Between The States on the Union side.

Both of us have "tamed" towns only to outlive our usefulness to those towns.

Both of us have achieved national if not world-wide "fame" for the identical reason—an ability to draw a revolver quickly and kill with it.

Both of us have appeared in the theatre in "self-exalting" plays, as he called them. We enjoyed discussing this particularly, laughing at the foolish things to which we were exposed. Our laughter, however, was not untinged with bitterness.

Inevitably, our conversation grew more solemn.

I discovered, to my surprise, that he believes in "life after death," and feels convinced that he has seen the ghosts of several of the men he has killed. His saying that disturbed me and I wonder now if what I have seen was really due to whiskey after all.

He suggested that I acquire and read a book on the subject of Spiritualism. I told him that I would, but I think I would rather not know if these things are true.

He also said that there is a woman here in Topeka who can "communicate" with the dead. That thought really chilled my blood and I changed the subject as soon as I could.

I told him about the man I had seen shot in Dawes. I said that seeing that body riddled with lead had made me aware, for the first time, of the fear and hatred with which I must be regarded.

Hickok nodded. He knew the feeling well, he said. I recall his exact words.

"We are victims of our notoriety," he said. "No longer men but figments of imagination. Journalists have endowed us with qualities which no man could possibly possess. Yet men hate us for these very nonexistent qualities."

His smile was sad.

"Our time is written on the sands, Mr. Halser," he said. "We are living dead men."

I believe that he is right. All this time, I have been telling myself that the skills I have to offer continue to be of value.

Now I wonder if this is so. It may be that the day of the so-called "gunfighter" is on the wane; that, soon, it will be little more than the memory of a brief period in time when masters of the handgun ruled the frontier.

A living dead man. That is what I have been for some time now.

The following night, Clay's marriage ended.

September 24, 1875

I wonder if fate had anything to do with what happened tonight. The facts seem to support the notion. More and more, I have this feeling that my life has been worked out by some one other than myself.

It is the first time I have ever eaten in Waltham's Restaurant.

It is the first time I have ever eaten lobster.

It is the first time I have had a belly ache in such a long time that I can not recall the last.

All these things combined to bringing me back to the hotel room hours earlier than usual.

I found Hazel in bed with some cow boy, both of them drunk.

"*Oh, my God,*" Hazel said when I unlocked the door and came into the room.

The cowboy stared at me in shock.

Then, I guess, he thought that I was going to kill him on the spot because he lunged from the bed and ran across the room, stark naked, going for his gun belt.

I did not shoot him. I kicked over the chair on which his gun belt hung. Then I hit him two or three times with the barrel of my revolver and threw him into the hallway the way he was. His clothes I threw out the window.

Hazel started crying and begging me to forgive her. She said that she was "lonely" with me gone all the time and needed a little "companionship."

I paid no attention to what she was saying. I got my bag from the closet and put my few belongings in. I felt grateful to her. She had made it easy for me to leave.

Not that she wanted me to leave. She kept hanging on to my arm, and crying, and begging me to forgive her, and stay.

Finally, when she saw that I was going to leave any way, she started cursing me and calling me a "no good, three-toed son of a b———" who had lost his "guts." She told me that she has been sleeping with "dozens" of cow boys while I was out gambling. She started to describe to me what she did with them. I had to hit her to shut her up. It was either that or kill her.

I am staying at the *Richmond Hotel* tonight. Tomorrow, I am going to leave Topeka and head West. I hope I never see Hazel again. I have accepted the fact that I am to be alone until the end, however soon or late that may come.

The following day, Clay entrained from Topeka and began his final "tour" of the West, if such a random peregrination can be called a tour.

He was like a man without a country now, incessantly on the move.

Everywhere he went, the result followed one of two patterns.

One: the town was "rough and ready" and, challenged, Clay was forced to talk or shoot his way out of trouble. Twice, he managed the former, once was compelled to perform the latter. On this occasion, he killed his opponent.

Two: the town was so domesticated that he felt uneasy and out of place. Here, the pressures against his life were replaced by pressures even harder to adjust to—the pressures of civilization crowding him out, making him extinct before his time.

He kept moving West.

One town he visited listed him as a vagrant and ordered him to leave within twenty-four hours. Enraged, he tore the notice off its board but, in a day, departed as requested.

In another town, suffering the effects of drink, he had to be hospitalized for two weeks.

In yet another town (Red Hill, Nebraska) he actually com-

*mitted himself to the job of local peace officer, then, after
making his "rounds" for one night, became so terrorized by a
rise of deep-seated dread within himself that he drank himself unconscious and, following a week-long bout of drinking, fled the town in ignominious defeat, thus ending, before
he started it, his resolve to "get back into living."*

*Finally, eschewing towns altogether, he spent the rest of the
winter "grub lining," riding from ranch to ranch and living
off them, a welcome guest because he brought, with him, news
of the "outside" world. During this time, reverting to an earlier notion, he introduced himself as Mr. Blackstone. Except
in one case, no one ever recognized him.*

*In February, he began to experience eye trouble and, after
ignoring it as long as he could, went to see a doctor in Julesberg, Colorado. There, he discovered that he had contracted
a venereal infection (probably from Hazel) and was in a me-
dian stage of gonorrheal ophthalmia. The doctor did what he
could for Clay but told him that, in course of time, blindness
was inevitable.*

*Clay remained in Julesberg for a week, uncertain as to his
plans, then, on a sudden impulse, decided to try some mining
and left for Silver Gulch.*

*I will comment no further. The rest of the tale speaks for
itself.*

April 18, 1876

I have arrived in Silver Gulch. If my eyes hold out, I am in
hopes of raising enough money to pay for Melanie's education. I will have it placed in a bank in Hickman in her name.
I will make sure that the money can not be used for anything
except her education. It is something I will do for her.

This town is certainly a crude place. There is only one,
narrow street filled with stumps, boulders, and logs. Dozens
of small, ugly saloons line the street, all made of raw pine, as
are the gambling halls and w———— houses. The street itself
is thick with wagons, houses, mules and ox teams. There

seems never a moment when there is not a haze of dust in the air.

I have taken a room at the one hotel here—*The Silver Lode*—a ramshackle building built of cheap, cracking wood. I have cleaned and shaved off my mustache. I look younger but not much.

I am sitting on the bed, making this entry. I am very tired. It has been a long trip and I am bone weary. My old wound is giving me "action" again and feels like a toothache in my right leg. Also, the foot hurts some. It is strange that I can *still* feel those missing toes once in a while when I am really tired!

I am going to take a nap now. Later, I will go out and have some supper and, perhaps, a game of cards.

Later: Back from supper. It is almost nine o'clock. I was going to play some cards but have lost the desire. I am tired and have no energy. I do not see how I can do any mining the way I feel.

What fool idea made me get all dressed, I wonder? My white, ruffled shirt and flowered waistcoat, my black string tie, black trousers, black cutaway, black sombrero and dark calf skin boots. Why here, in this God-forsaken place?

Why do I pretend? I shaved off the mustache and got all dressed up so that I would be recognized. I wrote "Clay Halser" on the hotel register and not Mr. Blackstone. It seems I can not live without recognition. I hate it but, like whiskey, it has become a weakness. Even knowing the pain it brings, I can not stay away from it.

It worked, of course. The hotel clerk had, undoubtedly, told everyone I was in town. When I came down he said, "Good evening, Mr. Halser." People in the street looked at me and some of them said, "Good evening, Mr. Halser." Many were surprised to see that I am still alive. They thought that I had died during the time I was grub lining.

And "he" was pleased. Poor Clay Halser in his gambler's dress, pleased to see that they knew him. Because there is nothing else left for him.

There is less than nothing left. Before I had finished supper, whatever pleasure I felt was taken from me.

Some local merchants approached with an offer of the City Marshal job. I told them I would think it over for a few days. I do not have to think it over for a second. I knew, before they were finished speaking, that I could not take the position. I have no will left any more. What happened in Red Hill is fresh in mind and humbles me. My City Marshal days are over despite my need for money.

Worse than that, my days for courage seem to be at an end too. After eating, I went to a saloon for a drink and a card game. I was told, by the bar tender, that a group of six men (three of them former employees of the Griffin Ranch) are threatening to kill me, saying that I am a murdering dog and back shooter.

I pretended to be amused. Soon afterward, however, I left and came back to the hotel room like a dog with my tail between my legs. I am afraid to meet them. After all the years of . . .

No, by God . . . !

Later: Victory that is not victory.

I am back in my room again. While making the earlier entry, I suddenly became enraged and vowed that I would rather die in a "blaze of glory" than hide in my room like a coward.

I put on my gun and went to the saloon I had been in. I asked the bar tender where the six men were and he told me that they had been hanging out in *Number 9 Saloon:* I left and started down the street followed by some people. At the time, I did not care. I was so mad. Now I know that they were following the *Hero of The Plains*, not a living man.

I went into *Number 9* and placed my back to the wall, unbuttoning my coat.

The six men were standing at the counter. I recognized two of them from the Griffin Ranch. My heart was pounding, but I managed to keep my voice clear because I was angry.

"I hear that you have been making threatening remarks

against me and I have come to give you your chance to kill me," I said.

The six men stared at me.

"Well?" I said. "Are you going to start shooting or shall I?"

They did not stir.

"If you are really brave and not just a pack of sneaking curs, you will give me a show right now!" I said.

They were statues.

"*Well?*" I shouted. "Go *on!*" I told them. I have not felt such fury since the night I badgered Jess Griffin. The strange thing is that I do not even know if it was really the six men I was angry at.

"Draw, you ————s!" I told them. I wanted them to fight me more than any thing I have ever wanted. I think I wanted them to kill me.

They would not draw.

"All right," I said. "Unbuckle your gun belts and hand them over."

They did it without a word. I picked them up with my left hand, keeping my revolver in my right.

"In the future," I said, "I suggest you wear skirts instead of guns."

With that I left the saloon amid the cheers of many. I dropped their guns into the first horse trough I came to and went back to the hotel. My moment of "glory."

I am sitting here, cold and shaking. What if they decided to come and get me? I could not hope to win. They would kill me in seconds.

I am just not up to these things any more. I have lost my nerve. There is nothing left inside me. I am empty.

Later: It is almost four o'clock in the morning.

I guess they are not going to come for me.

I know I can not sleep however.

I dozed off for a little while before and had another dream. A man without a face was drawing on me. My arm and head were like lead and I could scarcely move it. I woke up as death struck.

My mind is a turmoil of thoughts.

I have been thinking about Anne and Melanie. I have been thinking about Mr. Courtwright and those days in Hickman long ago. I have been thinking about Pine Grove and my family and Mary Jane. I have been thinking about Caldwell and Mayor Rayburn and Keller. I have been thinking about Henry and our days together. I have been thinking about Ben, and John, and Jim.

I have been thinking about all these things but I can not believe that any of them really happened. It is not that I can not believe that Henry, and Ben, and John, and Jim, and Mr. Courtwright are dead.

I can not believe that they ever lived.

I feel very odd. Out in the street, it is noisy. I hear some one singing. I hear a man curse. I hear a horse walking by. There is a snapping noise which I can not identify. I sit in this ugly room and think about myself. *Who am I?* I look at my body but it seems to be another man's. I look at my hand as it writes these words, but the hand seems to write by itself. Is it my hand? Are the words my words?

No memory is real. I try to catch one in my mind. They run like water. I can not hold a single, true remembrance. I do not think they ever existed. I can not believe in any thing but this room because it is all I can see. I do not think there is a Hickman, or that there is an Anne, or a Melanie. There is no Hays. No one ever lived or died there. I did not kill Ben because there never was a Ben. I did not hang Henry because no one named Henry ever lived.

I run on without purpose. The words I write are the words of a fool. Who am I to say that nothing is real? Every thing is real.

I am the one who is unreal.

April 19, 1876

It is after noon. I have slept too late. The pains in my leg and foot are bothering me. My back is stiff. The air is very damp.

I am going to get dressed and have some breakfast. Then I will find out about getting started with the mining. A lot of men are making a good raise here. The hills are full of silver. There is no reason why I can not get some for myself.

What a folly if I hit it rich and become a wealthy man!

It looks as though it may rain before the day is over.

More later.